ALL THE DAYS
WERE SUMMER

ALL THE DAYS WERE SUMMER

Robert Funderburk

Thorndike Press • Thorndike, Maine

Published in 1997 by arrangement with Bethany House Publishers.

Thorndike Large Print ® Christian Mystery Series.

The tree indicium is a trademark of Thorndike Press.

The text of this Large Print edition is unabridged.
Other aspects of the book may vary from the original edition.

Set in 16 pt. Plantin.

Printed in the United States on permanent paper.

Library of Congress Cataloging in Publication Data

Funderburk, Robert, 1942–
    All the days were summer / by Robert Funderburk.
      p.   cm.
    ISBN 0-7862-1233-0 (lg. print : hc : alk. paper)
    1. Large type books. I. Title.
  [PS3556.U59A79   1997b]
  813'.54—dc21
                                     97-35682

To
Henry Biggers.

A treasured part of my childhood
and my favorite preacher
since those days long ago.

And to
Inez, his wife.

"A virtuous woman.
The heart of her husband
doth safely trust in her."

Contents

Prologue

People remembered her eyes. Taken at first by her flawless olive complexion and placid face framed by the soft, dark sweep of her hair, they would smile and perhaps say a word or two of greeting to this child of obvious wealth and good breeding. Then most would, for some unknown reason, feel a vague uneasiness, then a sudden impulse to turn away . . . but not before they took that one last look. "Lovely, dark, and deep," a friend of her father's had once described them — eyes that revealed too much . . . or perhaps nothing at all.

She lived in a three-story house on Coliseum Street in the Garden District of New Orleans. When she awakened in the morning, and in the stillness of night just before she drifted off to sleep, she could hear the whine and rumble of the old iron streetcars out on St. Charles Avenue.

Painted white with green shutters, the narrow house rose above a brick walkway that ran from the front steps to the gate in the scrolled and feathered iron fence enclosing the property. Beneath the overhang of a magnolia tree, which stood like an ancient green sentinel in the side yard, galleries ran across the front and partway down the left side of the first two stories.

The men who came to see her father on business, often with fancy-dressed women clinging tightly to their arms, always used the side entrance. It opened into a foyer connected to a spacious office with a rosewood desk; heavy, dark furniture and bookcases; drapes of a burnished gold color; and lamps that gave the room the soft amber glow of perpetual twilight.

A tiny alcove beneath the stairs in the foyer proved to be the ideal playhouse for a five-year-old girl and her dolls. Her father, seldom home except to sleep and handle his confidential business appointments, had little time for raising a daughter. When he had visitors in his office, she would go to her playhouse to be near him and to hear the sound of his voice speaking with people she would never know.

"Gracious! How many cookies are you going to eat?" Wearing a pale blue dress with tiny pearl buttons and white piping, she sat on the gleaming cypress floor of the alcove as she talked to her doll. "It's a good thing

I baked a big batch. Now, this is your last one. We don't want you putting on weight."

"Do you like this ribbon in my hair? Mrs. Guillaume bought it for me. She says it matches my eyes." She poured a cup of imaginary tea for her doll.

"Be careful now. It's *very* hot." Placing the cup and saucer in front of her doll, the child continued with a smile that didn't quite reach her eyes. "Mrs. Guillaume's always telling me how pretty I am. Everybody does . . . well almost. You're very pretty, too . . . well, not like you were before —"

Why should I care what happens to him anyway? He's a nobody.

But he's been with us eleven years, and he's got a wife and three kids. Who's gonna look out for them?

He should have thought about them when he fouled up that land deal. You know how much money that cost me?

Yeah, I got the figures right here.

A sudden gust of wind howled around the eaves of the old house, followed by the first raindrops gently splashing on the leaves of the trees. Then a hard December rain began to fall, making a dull drumming sound high up on the roof. Tin-colored light spilled through the leaded glass of the side door.

The child glanced at the raindrops that

streaked down the window looking out onto the porch, then placed a big chocolate chip cookie on a tiny saucer and sat it in front of her doll. "Now don't get any crumbs on your dress. Daddy had it made special to look just like mine.

"Now look what you've done! All over your dress. You know what happened last time." She lifted the teapot and slowly poured its contents over the head of her doll. With the smile never leaving her face, she watched the imaginary hot tea run down the doll's face, past one staring glass eye and the empty, torn socket of the other.

PART ONE

Sunlight

1

Feathers

In the midnight stillness of Evangeline, a solitary figure stood on the bandstand, surveying the fairgrounds. Open blue tents popped softly in the night breeze. Empty chairs and tables waited patiently for the music and food and fun that the morning would bring. Suddenly, the dark-clad visitor leaped to the ground, paced off the distance to a live oak with quick, deliberate steps, and climbed nimbly up into the tree.

Five minutes later, the wraithlike form vaulted from a low spreading limb, ran with an effortless gait to a car parked next to the road, and slid behind the steering wheel. The car roared into a U-turn toward the ferry, its tires humming along the blacktop next to the bayou.

"Forget it, Susan. I'm too old to try that." Dylan St. John raked his dark hair back out of his eyes, then folded his arms across his chest and leaned against the trunk of one of the massive live oaks shading the Evangeline Fairgrounds. Dressed in faded Levi's and a short-sleeved khaki shirt with flap pockets, he turned his blue eyes on the skinny, hawk-nosed man kneeling inside the makeshift pen. Constructed of four-foot wire fencing nailed to two-by-fours that had been driven into the ground with a heavy maul, it stood close to the banks of the bayou.

The man dipped his hand into a shiny five-pound bucket of pure lard and spread it liberally on the pig, which had finally given up struggling against the ropes binding it between two stakes. The animal's coarse hair, thickly coated with the lard, gleamed in the afternoon sunlight.

"*Old?* You're not even thirty." Susan St. John, wearing white sandals and a sleeveless cotton dress the color of new clover, slipped her arm around her husband's waist and leaned against him. Pointing toward the pig with a slim finger she said, "Besides, you're six-one and a hundred and sixty-five pounds. That poor little pig's only two-and-a-half feet tall."

Dylan gazed down at Susan's upturned face, oval-shaped with finely drawn features. Her skin, as smooth and pale as porcelain, was marked by a single scar — a tiny white crescent at the left corner of her mouth. The scar gave her a fragile and vulnerable appearance that somehow made Dylan feel that she was never quite safe when he wasn't with her.

"C'mon, you can do it." Susan's dark hair fell in a pleasant disarray about her shoulders and her green eyes were filled with light as she urged Dylan on.

Glancing at Emile DeJean — his best friend, boss, and sheriff of Maurepas Parish — Dylan said, "Okay, you win. But Emile's got to get in there with me."

Emile ran his hand through his curly black hair, flecked with gray. Two inches shorter than Dylan, with broad shoulders and a thick chest, Emile looked as though he could have swung a mean cutlass with Jean Lafitte's band of pirates who had roamed the swamps and bays further south. Even in his sun-faded khakis and white Izod shirt, Emile gave the appearance of a man who was not quite at home in his own century.

"I know you heard me, Emile." Dylan pressed the issue, not willing to be the sheriff department's solitary jester.

Emile smiled, his teeth shining white in contrast with his dark face, and began shaking his head slowly back and forth. "I'm on the wrong side of fifty for games like chase-the-pig. Besides, Emmaline wouldn't want me to get hurt."

"Oh, that little pig's not going to hurt you." Emmaline DeJean, a short, vital woman in her late forties, slipped through the crowd and handed Susan one of the paper cones of pink cotton candy she had gone to the midway to buy.

"Thanks," Susan said, taking a tuft of the cotton candy and biting into its airy substance. "I don't think I've had one of these since the last time Dylan took me to Pontchartrain Beach."

Emmaline rested her hand on her ample hip, a mischievous light in her warm brown eyes. "I really believe you can take him, Emile." She winked at Susan. "He may be a little smarter, but you're a lot stronger . . . and meaner."

Staring at the greasy, red-eyed pig, Emile said, "Well, with that vote of confidence from my wife, how could I lose? You ready, Dylan?"

"You're serious about this?" Dylan followed Emile's eyes toward the pig. Then he grinned at the dozen or so teenagers waiting to enter the gate and take part in the pig-chasing contest. "You boys make sure that thing doesn't get ahold of me now."

Susan and Emmaline, taking careful bites

of cotton candy, stood next to the fence watching Dylan and Emile follow the young men into the pen. A crowd began to gather as word got around that Evangeline's sheriff had entered the greased-pig contest. Fishermen, trappers, store clerks, waitresses, sugarcane farmers, and a lawyer or two threw their barbs from outside the fence.

"Hey, Emile! Ain't you kinda old to be playing chase wid' dat little pig?"

"Das' right. I thought we paid you all dat tax money for chasin' crooks."

"Looks like they greased the wrong *pig* to me." A tall, bearded man who obviously enjoyed the current fad of calling policemen "pigs," stuck his hands into the pockets of his bell-bottomed jeans and nodded at Emile.

Emile stared at the man, then remembered that he had arrested him on a simple drunk charge a few weeks before. He responded to the man's scowl with a pleasant smile.

Suddenly, Emile's heckler found himself face-to-face with a burly trapper from the Atchafalaya Basin. The trapper wore a pair of brand-new bib overalls and scuffed brogans and had a hunting knife the size of a small sword strapped to his side. His dark eyes blazed as he looked down at the heckler.

The heckler glanced nervously around,

started to say something, then turned abruptly and slouched away toward the Ferris wheel, bumper cars, and merry-go-round on the other side of the midway.

Watching the little drama play out before her, Susan found in it yet another reason to be glad that she and Dylan had moved down from Baton Rouge to the sleepy little river town of Evangeline. The fierce loyalty of the Cajuns for their own people, she thought, kept alive a quality that was fading from most of American life. The late sixties seemed to have begun a gradual eroding of the sense of family and community that had been one of the cornerstones of her country's strength. On this May morning in the first year of the following decade the current trend seemed alive and well, except in a few enclaves of the past like Evangeline.

A loud squealing sound disturbed Susan's thoughts. She turned to see the terrified pig bolt away as a boy tried to tackle it — coming away with nothing but a face full of grease.

The pig ran to the far corner of the pen with the younger boys in hot pursuit. Susan noticed Dylan and Emile giving each other hand signals as they walked behind the yelling gang. At the far corner, the pig suddenly broke through the line that had formed around it and headed straight for Dylan and Emile.

Emile pointed to his left. "Watch him over there. I've got him covered over here." Emile widened his stance for balance and leaned forward, arms opened to tackle the charging pig.

"I've got this side," Dylan shouted. He crouched down, his arms spread wide, bouncing back and forth on the balls of his feet in readiness.

Seizing the opportunity, Dylan dove headlong for the pig. He got one hand on its back leg, but it slipped through his clawing fingers like quicksilver. Dylan sprawled across the lawn. Shrieking in fear, the pig lowered its head and rushed Emile, who stood his ground. As the pig closed the distance between them, Emile bent over and grabbed for him with both arms. As his burly arms grazed the pig, it squealed loudly. The pig's rough bristles whisked right on through his would-be captor's legs, leaving them coated with thick white grease. Its hind foot clipped Emile on the ankle, sending him sprawling backward onto the grass.

The boys, shouting at their fallen comrades in the pig war, galloped past on the heels of the terrified animal.

"Pig-2, sheriff's department-0," one of the boys taunted.

"Hey, Sheriff, maybe you could get LSU to *sign* that pig! He'd make a great running back."

Dylan sat up, arms resting on his knees as he grinned over at Emile. "Look, somebody got him!"

A boy of nineteen, his neat tan slacks and navy pull-over shirt hardly wrinkled, had merely waited near the gate, knowing that the pig would elude the first rush of attackers and return to its starting point. When the terrified animal ran into a fence post, he simply bent over, braced his legs, and lifted it off the ground while it was still dazed.

Emile leaned back on his elbows, his khakis stained, arms shining with grease. "Guess you got to be smarter than a pig to catch one."

Beneath an open blue canopy set up as a dining area, Dylan sat in a folding chair next to Susan. Emile and Emmaline sat across from them at one of the long tables covered with a white cloth. Styrofoam plates piled with food, along with red paper cups of Coke, sat in front of them.

Close by, beneath the live oaks draped with hanging moss, a four-man band — two fiddles, an accordion, and drums — played "Colinda." Couples in shorts and jeans and summer shirts, wearing sandals or tennis shoes or going barefoot, bounced and twirled the Cajun two-step, using that peculiar bent-knee stomp on the hard-packed, dusty ground. The smells of boiled peanuts, fresh popcorn, cracklin's frying in a huge black pot, and the spicy gumbos and jambalayas cooking on butane stoves permeated the mild spring air.

"I wonder who made this crawfish etouf-fee?" Dylan asked as he forked some of the richly seasoned crawfish, red gravy, and rice mixture into his mouth. He savored the ex-quisite taste — created only with patience and long years of experience in the art of Cajun cooking.

Emmaline looked up from her plate of fried catfish smothered with crabmeat. "You know I made that, Cher. Seemed like I was in the kitchen half of last week fixing it." She stared at the piece of warm French bread in her hand as though a message had been printed on its brown, crusty side. "You know, sometimes I think I'll just start buying it frozen. It just takes too much time to fix dishes like that if you want to do it right."

Smiling at Susan, Emile shook his head slowly, "She's been saying that for years —

23

every fair, every family get-together." He turned to his wife. "Emma, you know better than I do that you'd never be satisfied with anybody's cooking but your own." Sipping steaming dark coffee from a Styrofoam cup, he added, "Neither would the rest of us — and *the rest of us* is a whole bunch of Cajuns who love your cooking."

Emmaline used her white plastic fork to emphasize her point. "I just might . . . someday."

Emile shook his head again, then turned to Susan. "How's little Dylan Jr. doing today?"

Susan unconsciously placed her hand on her stomach. "Progressing quite well, thank you, but he's making me a little nauseous first thing in the morning."

"I know just how you feel," Emile grinned. "His daddy has that same effect on me."

Dylan ignored Emile's remark, chewing slowly as he watched the band finish their number with a flourish.

"I don't mind that so much," Emile continued, "as long as he doesn't make half the politicians in South Louisiana want to nail our hides to the barn."

"One little phone call, Emile," Dylan defended himself. "And Ralph Raburn's not a politician."

"But he's tight with the governor, and he's going places in politics."

"And he knows something about what happened to Remy and those other kids."

Emile's face darkened. "You may be right, but he's not going to tell *you* anything." He stared at the streamer of Spanish moss, gleaming in the afternoon sunlight, lifting slightly in the breeze. "I want to find out what happened to those children as much as you do, Dylan, but you can't start at the top. You got to find out the hard way — from the bottom up."

Dylan nodded his agreement, knowing that Emile was right. He thought of Remy Batiste and his brother Russel, and of the other children he didn't know who had somehow disappeared in Louisiana's system of state corrections and welfare. In six months no law enforcement agency had made any substantial progress in finding any of them. Now they existed only as social summaries and psychological evaluations inside their manila case folders tucked away neatly inside green file cabinets.

Anger rising inside him, Dylan remembered the last time he had seen Remy — in the dank dark cell with its battered bunk, his shoulders stooped with the weight of his youth as surely as an old man's by the weight of age, his brown eyes filled with a sorrow far too deep for his fifteen years.

"The FBI's in on it now." Emile stated his office's official position. "All we can do is keep plugging away and hope we get a break on it sooner or later."

Dylan nodded, but the official status of the case didn't keep him from waking in the night with Remy's face looming before him like a plea from all the children lost somewhere in America.

"Now here comes a politician who never offends *anybody*," Emile announced.

"Maybe bore you to death," Emmaline added, "but he certainly won't offend you."

Dylan watched Dickie Breaux, Evangeline's mayor, climb the steps onto the bandstand. He wore a light blue seersucker suit, a canary yellow tie, and waved to the crowd with the straw bowler he carried in one hand. He had gained forty pounds since his days as a fighter pilot in Korea, but his smile was still youthful and full of gleaming white teeth on his tanned face.

Lifting the microphone off its heavy stand, Breaux opened his speech as he always did, *"Laissez les bon temps rouler,"* Cajun French for "Let the good times roll."

And as always, the crowd repeated his words, cheering and applauding Breaux, who had not only adopted the words as his opening remarks for most of his speeches but had embraced them as a way of life.

Breaux motioned for quiet, then turned on the syrup mill. "It's good to see so many of my friends out here today celebrating our Cajun way of life: eating, dancing, renewing old acquaintances, and in general, 'passing a good time.'"

Dylan smiled at Breaux's smooth style and watched the faces of the people as the mayor made each of them feel like his best friend. Suddenly the sound of Breaux choking crackled through the microphone.

Feathers? Dylan thought how absurd Breaux looked with a tight clump of gray and white turkey feathers protruding from his throat. Then he saw the shaft of the ancient arrow as Evangeline's mayor collapsed to the wooden floor of the bandstand.

Mass shock stunned the crowd for an instant, then screams pierced the mild afternoon. Women grabbed for their children as men glanced in all directions, trying to fend off any danger to their families.

Dylan saw four or five people converging on the bandstand. Among them were a local doctor and his nurse. Then his eyes locked on Emile's for an instant before they both instinctively turned toward the flight path of the arrow. In the deep shade of a live oak down at the bayou's edge, a shadowy figure vaulted to the ground from a low-spreading limb and ran with an effortless gait toward the road that parallelled the water's edge.

Fumbling in Susan's purse, Dylan grabbed his .38 revolver and turned toward the bayou. In his periphery, he saw Emile running toward the parking lot and the white Blazer with the gold Maurepas Parish Sheriff's Office emblem on the door.

"Be careful!"

Susan's words sounded as out of place as the feathers in Breaux's throat, Dylan thought as he sprinted across the hard ground. *Like something my mother used to tell me when I'd leave on a Friday night date.* When he reached the tree, Dylan stopped, took a breath, and peered around it. A dark blue Chevy Super Sport sat on the grassy bank between the road and the reeds and cattails lining the bayou. A slim figure in dark clothing tossed a crossbow into the backseat and slipped behind the wheel.

Resting his arm against the side of the tree for stability, Dylan grasped the .38 firmly with both hands and brought the sight to bear on the dark form behind the driver's window. He squeezed off a round, the blast ringing in his ears. A frosty patch of glass

28

brightened the center of the rear side window where his bullet punctured it. Then he pulled the little pistol back down, realigning the sights, and squeezed off another shot.

But the Chevy's engine had roared to life. Its tires spun wildly as the Chevy fishtailed on the spring clover, then shrieked as they hit blacktop, leaving twin trails of gray smoke rising from the burning lines of rubber.

The white Blazer bounced across a ditch between the fairgrounds and the blacktop, slipped sideways as Emile fought the wheel for control, then roared along the bayou. Dylan raced across the open ground, jumped the ditch and crossed the road in front of the speeding Blazer. Stomping on the brakes, Emile skidded to a stop just long enough for Dylan to jerk the door open and leap inside, then gunned the big engine. Shells along the roadside spanged off the truck's bottom as Emile picked up speed.

Emile cradled the microphone of the radio in his left hand. "Elaine, give me a NET on this channel. We're in pursuit. Mayor has been shot by an unknown suspect, small build and wearing dark clothing. He's driving a dark blue Chevy Super Sport and armed with some kind of a crossbow. Be sure to get Lonnie and A.J. on this thing as soon as you contact them. They're supposed to be on a stakeout somewhere west of White Castle. Tell them to take 404 east. They just might cut this guy off where it hits Highway 75."

Dylan pictured Elaine Lebeau, Emile's secretary, wearing her deputy's uniform complete with trousers and black boots. She'd be calmly and efficiently mobilizing the Maurepas Parish Sheriff's Office, contacting the deputies on patrol as well as those off duty, and giving directions over the radio as she traced the highways on the big map tacked to the wall next to her desk.

As Emile signed off, Dylan clicked the knob to 30.4, the state police band, and grabbed the microphone. "Troop A — this is MP-1. Mayor Breaux has been shot —"

"Tell them we want a BOLO on this," Emile interrupted, glancing at Dylan, then gazed back at the white lines speeding by on the blacktop in front of him.

"A *what?*"

"Be On the Look Out — BOLO," Emile explained. "Give the description."

"SP dispatcher," Dylan continued, "we want a BOLO on a late-model dark blue Super Sport, three miles west of Evangeline, heading west. . . ."

Grabbing the wheel with both hands, Emile leaned into the big looping curve where the road tracked the course of the bayou. The Blazer skidded slightly, tires crying on the asphalt surface, then found traction and straightened out of the curve. In the distance, on a long straightaway, the dark blue Chevy continued to pull away from them, then was lost around another turn.

"It oughta be against the law to make cars that fast." Emile squinted into the afternoon sunlight streaming through the windshield. His hands clutched the steering wheel in the ten-past-ten position. "We don't stand a chance against that 396 engine in a lightweight chassis like that."

Finished with the radio, Dylan shoved the mike back into its niche. "All we have to do is stay as close as we can behind him and let Sonny and A. J. block off the road between Bayou Sorrel and Pigeon."

"If Elaine gets ahold of them in time."

"Even if she doesn't, one of the state police units should be able to get there." Dylan saw the speedometer needle rocking past one hundred twenty. The wind screamed by the windows of the Blazer, louder than the whine of the engine.

Slowing to navigate the curve where they had lost sight of the Chevy, Emile fought against the shuddering, bucking motion of the Blazer. Then, reaching the next straight-

31

away, he once again floored the accelerator.

The tall reeds and cattails growing along the bayou swayed in the wind created by the Blazer as it sped by. The blue Super Sport, idling in the black shade of a huge gum tree screened from the road by tall grass and the shimmering green cascade of several willows, pulled slowly out into the sunlight, then headed back toward Evangeline.

"How could I be so stupid?" Emile, still wearing his faded khakis and white knit shirt, leaned against a battered table shoved into a corner outside the door of his office. He spooned sugar into a thick white mug of coffee.

Elaine sat at her desk, cluttered with maps and folders and messages on slips of pink paper. She wore her deep red hair pulled back in a French braid. Although in her early thirties, the scattering of freckles across her face gave her a girlish appearance. "Don't be too hard on yourself, Chief. You didn't have many options." She glanced at Dylan. "Besides, it's hard to spot anything at a hundred and twenty miles an hour."

"I should have seen where he pulled off the road," Dylan offered, "but all that's not going to help us catch him. I might go talk to the ferry captain again — see if maybe he can remember at least part of the number on the license plate."

"Won't help," Emile said, taking a sip of coffee. "Lonnie and A. J. got everything he knew. All he saw was a blue Super Sport with a driver wearing dark clothes and a black baseball cap. The deckhand would have been our best bet, but he didn't remember anything." He shook his head slowly. "Doesn't surprise me though. The way they both hit the bottle, there's gonna be a real tragedy out on that river some day."

"What can you do?" Elaine shrugged. "They got their jobs with political pull, and this is South Louisiana."

Dylan sat down on the edge of a heavy green table pushed against the side of Elaine's desk to form a U-shaped work area with the wall on the other side. "Sorry I fumbled things on the radio, calling in the chase to the state police, Emile."

Emile dismissed the apology with a wave of his hand. "Don't worry about it. You've only been on the job a few weeks. It takes a long time to learn procedures and all that law-enforcement jargon."

Dylan nodded. His thoughts had already drifted off in another direction. He saw again the shadowy figure leaping down from the huge live oak limb; saw the smooth gait of

33

the runner on the way to the Chevy. Something stirred at the back of his mind — something that began to nudge a memory out into the light. . . .

"You didn't hear a thing from Troop C or B, Elaine?" Emile had already asked the question earlier but had lost recollection in the whirl of thoughts as he tried to figure out all the possible escape routes.

"No, Chief."

"Well, that means he got wherever he was going before we realized that he'd given us the slip. He might have made it down to New Orleans, or up to Baton Rouge, or maybe somehow slipped by us and on down to Thibodaux."

His train of thought interrupted by Emile's comments, Dylan tried to pull the lost memory to the front of his mind, but the chance was gone.

2

A Cajun Wife

The steeple of the little white frame church gleamed in the morning sunlight. Cars were parked at random on the grounds in the shade of the oaks and black gums and sycamores. Clumps of purple water hyacinths and islands of lily pads floated out on the dark surface of the bayou.

"You thought he might actually show up here at the funeral?" Dylan, wearing a dark suit and tie, stood next to Emile in the shadowy entrance of the church, gazing out at the remaining mourners in the graveyard.

Emile loosened his black tie and pinched the bridge of his nose with thumb and forefinger. "You never can tell. It happens sometimes."

"You didn't see any strangers, though," Dylan pondered out loud. "Nobody suspicious-looking."

A wry smile flickered on Emile's face. "I saw some strangers, all right." He glanced at

35

a young woman in a black dress and a hat with a veil that partially covered her face. She was picking her way gingerly on high heels among the tilting old tombstones on the way to her car. "But they were all ladies," Emile added, pointing toward the graveyard. "Like that one over there hiding her face behind black net."

Dylan glanced at the slim woman in black. "I heard rumors that Dickie had a way with the women."

Emile nodded. "There were at least seven or eight here today that I'd never seen before."

"Jealous husband?" Dylan asked as he watched the woman in black climb into a long, white Cadillac.

"Could be," Emile replied flatly. "We've got to check out any leads in that direction for sure."

Dylan gazed at the elegant automobile with its liveried driver while it bumped slowly along the shell-covered drive, leaving a thin white powdery cloud in its wake.

Emile turned to go inside and took a seat in the last row. More than a hundred years old, the church pews were made of heart cypress from deep in the Atchafalaya Basin. Gleaming dully in colored light slanting in through the stained-glass windows, the pews had become like family members for generations of people who had attended the little community church.

Dylan sat down across the aisle from Emile. Emile's face gave off an appearance of pain. "You all right?" Dylan asked his friend.

"Huh?" Emile rubbed the back of his neck, his dark eyes glinting like anthracite in the dim light. "Sure. I'm fine."

Dylan knew the various clues were starting to come together in Emile's mind. Emile seldom spoke without considering his words, except in jest. *That's a lesson I could learn from him.*

"Something occurred to me while the priest was handling the funeral arrangements," Emile said as he stared at the ornate candlesticks on the altar. "Maybe it had something to do with the . . . antiquity of the mass . . . the robes and chalice and all that."

Dylan waited for the second shoe to fall, but his patience had a half-life of about three seconds. "What?"

"About six months ago another mayor was killed. I should have put it together easily . . . but I didn't." Emile shook his head slowly before adding, "Guess I'm getting senile."

Dylan leaned forward, resting his arms on

his knees. "Will you please tell me what you're talking about?"

"The mayor of Pierre Part . . . it's a little community —"

"I know," Dylan cut in, "just north of Lake Verrett. Now, what about the mayor?"

"He's not even a real mayor. Everybody just calls him that. He was killed by a sword. The coroner said it was a heavy iron weapon, not a saber or anything that modern — more like a broadsword."

"You mean Arthur, Lancelot, Knights of the Round Table . . . that kind of sword?"

Emile studied his shoes and said, "I didn't think much of it at the time when I saw the report, but now with this crossbow murder —"

"It's one of the old-type bolts, too," Dylan added. "Wood shaft instead of fiberglass, iron-tipped instead of steel, real feathers and not those plastic imitations." Through the bottom of the windows made of clear glass, he watched the breeze wrinkling the surface of the bayou. "I think pretty soon everything in our lives but the food we eat's going to be made out of plastic . . . or something like it."

Dylan stood up, paced slowly down the aisle, then returned. "So what we've got here is a Camelot killer. Somebody who thinks he's on a crusade against who knows what?"

Emile shook his head. "Don't rush things. It's too soon to start making assumptions like that."

"Where do we go from here?"

"Lonnie and A. J. have already started. I've got them questioning everybody along the route we figure the suspect took from Highway 75, where he gave us the slip, to the ferry landing, and north and south on the river road where he left the ferry. It's gonna be slow going; gonna take a lot of legwork. Maybe they can find one or two of the other ferry passengers that day to talk to. One of them might remember something."

"And?"

"And the state police are already checking all the dark blue Super Sports in the state, but that's gonna take a long time. Besides, it could have been repainted, might even be from another state; a real long shot."

"And?" Dylan prompted again.

"And the girlfriends. That's where *you* come in. From what I've heard of Dickie, it's quite a list — a list we don't have, if one even exists."

"How am I gonna find all these girlfriends?"

Emile rose from the pew and stepped toward the bright entrance of the church.

"Same as anybody else: legwork."

"Just point me in the right direction."

"Easy. The first one is, anyway. You can start with Janet."

"Who?"

"His ex-wife. You know her."

Dylan gave him a puzzled look. "I don't know any *Janet Breaux*."

"She took her maiden name back — Cloud."

"Janet Cloud? That nice lady that works over at the Clerk of Court's office. She was married to Dickie Breaux?"

"Yep."

"I took her for having better sense than that," Dylan mused.

"It's not that unusual. A lot of nice, sensible women end up with goofy husbands."

"You think so? Name one."

Emile shot a sly glance in Dylan's direction. "Susan St. John comes to mind."

"Since Robert got killed, I hardly *ever* get to see my own grandchildren!" Emmaline, wearing a pearl gray dress and a frown born of a grandmother's righteous anger, rested her hands lightly on the steering wheel of her 1956 Ford. Two-tone blue and white and in mint condition, it had turned only 73,000 miles.

40

Susan peered into the mirror on the flip side of a sun visor, fluffing her dark hair with her fingertips, then pushed the visor back into place and smoothed the collar of her lavender blouse. She knew that Emmaline and Emile were still trying to come to terms with their son's death in the Tet Offensive in Vietnam two years before. "Are they still living in Dallas?"

Emmaline nodded. "It might as well be Singapore, though. Since Mary got remarried, she acts like Emile and I don't exist anymore."

"I'm sure she doesn't do it intentionally, Emma. It just seems like there's not enough time these days. Everybody's always in such a hurry, and I'm sure it must be a real madhouse in a big city like Dallas."

"Maybe so. . . ." Emmaline had known Susan for two or three years, but the two women had grown closer since Susan and Dylan moved to Evangeline. "I'm glad you and Dylan moved here, Susan. With Robert gone and Anne in New Orleans most of the time, my maternal instincts have been on a leave of absence. I think I might just adopt you."

Susan smiled, her cheeks coloring slightly. "You might end up asking for a refund. I'm kind of moody sometimes, and I just *hate* housework."

"I knew there was something else I liked about you," Emmaline said, grinning.

"I'm glad we left Baton Rouge. I only had one close friend, a lady I used to teach with," Susan reflected. "Evangeline already seems like home. People are almost like family down here — most of them, anyway."

"We do look out for each other," Emmaline agreed as she jerked the wheel to the left, avoiding a gray cat that had darted out into her path. With a sigh of relief, she continued, "Births, weddings, sickness, funerals . . . the good times and the bad."

Susan felt her gray slacks fitting more tightly around her waist. "I hope the doctor won't think I've put on too much weight."

Emmaline gave her an oblique glance. "Are you kidding? You *needed* to put on some weight."

"I've put on ten pounds, and I'm only four months along."

"Don't worry about it," Emmaline said, dismissing any concern with a flick of her wrist. "There's more to life than trying to make your doctor happy." She reached over, encircling Susan's upper arm with her thumb and forefinger. "Besides, you're still too skinny for a Cajun wife. What you need is a few more oyster po'boys, a muffuletta or two, some Bananas Foster, and a slice of pecan pie."

"Is that the way you get to be a Cajun wife?"

Emmaline laughed and said, "That's part of it, sugar. Down here we believe in good food, hard work, and harder play."

"You've had two children, Emma."

"That's a fact."

"Is the pain really that bad?"

Emmaline gave Susan a merry smile. "Nothing to it, sugar. They've got a thing called an epidural."

"You mean like a spinal?" Susan asked.

"That's it," Emmaline grinned. "They could boil you in oil and you wouldn't feel a thing."

"Well, that's a relief. I was kind of worried about it." Susan straightened up in her seat, holding her chin a little higher. "Not much, you understand, but a little bit."

"Your mother never talked to you about what to expect with childbirth?"

Susan rubbed her hands together, then folded them in her lap. "We . . . uh, don't really get together very much anymore." She glanced at the old railroad bridge, speckled with rust, as they crossed Evangeline Bayou.

"Why not?"

"She and Daddy don't approve of Dylan."

Emmaline merely shrugged and said, "Hmmm," as though the matter was worth no further discussion.

"Do you ever wish you'd had more children, Emma?" Susan wondered why she had asked the question as soon as the words left her mouth.

Rubbing her fingertip alongside her small, slightly upturned nose, Emma said, "I hadn't really thought much about it before . . . before we lost Robert." Her brown eyes softened, but her voice carried a thin hoarseness. "Now sometimes I think it would be nice to have another son around."

Another thought formed itself into words before Susan considered it. "Dylan won't talk about the war very much. The last time I asked him to tell me something about what he had done over there, he said the whole thing was just a fraternity prank that got out of hand and now all the newspapers and TV networks have to play along with it."

Emmaline's eyebrows raised a quarter of an inch as she looked over at Susan, then she began to chuckle softly. Nodding her head, she said, "That sounds like something Dylan would come up with."

"Sometimes I think the older he gets, the crazier he gets," Susan responded. "He makes a joke out of anything."

"That's one way to get by in this ol' world, baby," Emmaline chuckled again. "It's dangerous to take things too seriously — especially yourself."

Susan stared out the window at the sugarcane fields stretching to a distant treeline, lying flat and fallow in the spring sunshine. "Sometimes he wakes up at night in a cold sweat. But he says he never remembers his dreams."

"He remembers," Emmaline said flatly. "He just doesn't want to talk about what he remembers."

"How do you —"

"Emile fought in North Africa. He was there with Patton's Tank Corps in '43."

"He won't tell you anything?"

"After twenty-five years, he opened up a little," Emmaline murmured, blinking away a tear. "The first time was two years ago, not long after Robert was killed."

"I'm sorry I brought this up, Emma. I don't even know why I did."

"No, it's all right," Emmaline assured her. "I think sometimes it helps to have someone to talk to. Just a few words seems to make it easier to handle." She cleared her throat. "Talking makes what happened real, something you can deal with — not like when you're all by yourself and the memories just come at you, and there's nothing you can do about them."

Susan wondered what dreams still haunted Dylan; what dark and lethal memories followed him in his sleep, taking him unaware in those times when he awakened, his skin cold and clammy.

"You got a name picked out for the baby?" Emma asked, obvious in her attempt to move the conversation back onto cheerful ground.

Rubbing the corners of her eyes, Susan climbed out of her thoughts. "Erin."

"Erin St. John." Emmaline tested the sound of the name. "I like that. Is it a family name?"

"No, we just liked it."

"What if it's a boy?"

"Dylan, I think."

Emmaline tilted her head toward Susan, the corners of her eyes crinkling with mischief. "You really think you can live with *two* Dylan St. Johns?"

"Hmmm . . . never thought about it quite that way." Susan pursed her red lips, a pensive look in her eyes. "Herman — now there's a nice name. Herman St. John. Has a certain flair, don't you think?"

Their laughter filled the car.

Dylan St. John knew Janet Cloud to be a

very punctual woman. She would leave the courthouse every day at two o'clock and walk the three blocks to her house for afternoon tea. She had filed many of Dylan's Bills of Information — "True and Corrects," she had called them — when he was in probation and parole, and she knew the workings of the Clerk of Court's office like he knew the grip for a topspin backhand.

The clock set into the dashboard of the 1965 Ford sheriff's unit read exactly two o'clock when Dylan parked across the street from Janet Cloud's house. At five minutes after two she turned the corner and moved with a sprightly step down the sidewalk toward her home. Janet Cloud was a handsome woman. She wore a long print skirt in pastel shades of green and blue and a pale green blouse. Her auburn hair, streaked with gray, was worn up, and her reading glasses hung around her neck on a chain that swayed with each step she took.

Dylan got out of the car and called to her as she started up the walk to her front porch. "Miss Cloud —"

Janet turned, squinted slightly, and smiled as she recognized who it was calling to her.

"Can I have a few minutes of your time?"

"*May*, Dylan," she corrected him. "*May*,

47

not *can*. Of course you may. Come on in. I'll fix us some tea."

Dylan stopped himself from making a face at the thought of tea, which he had never developed a taste for, but spending time with Janet Cloud over a cup of tea seemed like a pleasant enough way of getting the information he needed. In spite of feeling like a schoolboy being mildly scolded for bad grammar, he nodded and smiled.

Hurrying over to her, Dylan said, "I hope I didn't catch you at a bad time."

Janet continued up the walk. "As you already know, I use this time every day as my respite from the maddening crowd," she pointed toward the courthouse, "but since you're such a sincere young man, I'll make an exception."

"Thanks." In the presence of Janet Cloud, Dylan always felt like an actor playing a part without a copy of the script. He followed her up the steps to the wide front porch. A swing made of cypress weathered to a silver gray hung from the high ceiling by galvanized chains. "You've got a nice place here," he commented while he waited for her to unlock the heavy oak door, constructed with leaded glass insets.

"I grew up here." Janet pushed the door

open. "It's been in the family for generations."

Dylan briefly pictured the home of his own childhood in Algiers, a working-class neighborhood across the Mississippi River from New Orleans. He followed her into the house.

Laying her purse and keys on the marble shelf of a hall tree, Janet motioned Dylan toward a long mahogany table in the dining room. "Make yourself at home." She stepped over to a console stereo against the wall, opened the lid, selected a record, and placed it on the turntable.

Dylan glanced at the album cover as she laid it aside. It read, "Mendelssohn's Violin Concerto in E Minor." As the first few notes played, he asked, "That's Mendelssohn, isn't it? One of his violin concertos."

Janet raised an eyebrow. "You know classical music?"

"Just a bit."

"Well," her lips curved slightly as she glanced at the album cover laying on the record cabinet, "enjoy the music then. I'll only be a few minutes." She turned in a smooth motion and continued on into the kitchen.

Dylan pulled out a high-backed chair and sat down. He gazed at the high windows bordered by lacy curtains that reminded him of his grandmother's. With no light on in the room, it was filled with shadows and streaked with sunlight. As the clean, elegiac sound of violins drifted through the room, he wondered what it would have been like to have been brought up in this home.

"I have thirty minutes, Dylan," Janet noted as she carried a bamboo tray holding two steaming cups and a sugar-and-cream service. On the tray were scones and tea cakes on a silver-rimmed saucer. After placing the items on the table, she sat down across from Dylan.

While Dylan prepared himself to down his tea without making a face, he noticed that one of the cups held coffee.

"I remembered you don't like tea," Janet said, reaching for the cream pitcher. "Perhaps you'd better tell me why you're here." She poured cream into her cup and stirred, the spoon clinking on the saucer as she lay it down. "I have a feeling that it wasn't just to have tea with an old woman."

Looking into the clear green eyes enshrined in her patrician face, Dylan tried to imagine Janet Cloud twenty-five years earlier. "You may be the most attractive woman in this parish, Miss Cloud. I can associate you with a lot of things; old isn't one of them."

"It isn't necessary to flatter me, Dylan," Janet chided as she held her cup poised in the air. "I *always* cooperate with the authorities. And besides, you're a nice boy."

Again, Dylan felt like a ten-year-old. "I didn't mean to offend you."

"Oh, you didn't! I rather enjoyed it." She closed her eyes slowly, then opened them and blinked. "It reminded me of Richard when we were both young and foolish. He was always quick with a compliment. Of course, he got older like all of us — but he remained foolish."

"There's certainly nothing foolish about you."

"No," Janet agreed. "Most everyone agrees that I'm very sensible — except of course for marrying Richard."

"We *are* talking about Dickie Breaux, our mayor, aren't we?"

"Ex-mayor," Janet corrected him. "Yes, we are. I never could bring myself to call him Dickie. Sometimes I think if he'd insisted on being called Richard, like I suggested, he might have had a chance at becoming an adult."

"How long were you married?"

"Twenty years. Probably because he was

away so much of the time with his air force duties."

"Was he a pilot?"

"Yes, and an excellent one, too — or so I'm told. But when we moved back here he couldn't change his lifestyle from hot-shot pilot back to hometown boy."

Dylan noticed that Janet's eyes seemed to veil over as she spoke of her dead husband.

"Well, it wasn't long before his marriage vows ran headlong into his indiscretions. Evangeline isn't the place to live if you're a professional philanderer," she said as she clinked her cup into the saucer. "But I have a daughter and son-in-law in Atlanta and two lovely grandchildren, so I'm content."

"Dickie's . . . fondness for the ladies didn't stop him from getting elected mayor," Dylan said almost as a question.

Janet's face formed an expression of mild surprise. "This is South Louisiana, Dylan," she said as if that were sufficient explanation — and it was.

"How long were you back here before you separated?" Dylan felt uneasy having to question Janet about the recent death of her husband.

"About a year."

He remembered the way she looked at

the funeral: dressed in black, pale, her eyes red and swollen from crying, yet elegant in her grief. "I'm sorry to have to question you like this, Miss Cloud, but it has to be done."

"I know you're on official business, Dylan, but we're not in the courthouse . . . so could you call me Janet? You're making me feel like somebody's spinster aunt."

"Sure," Dylan agreed. Spooning sugar into his almost forgotten coffee, he stirred and took a swallow. "We're looking for somebody with a reason to kill Dickie," he said, thinking of no way he could phrase the question to make it less painful.

Janet gave him a strange, sad smile. "As you probably know by now, everybody loved Richard — except perhaps for a few jealous boyfriends or husbands."

Dylan stared into his coffee, then met Janet's eyes. "That's where the investigation is taking us. . . ." The haunting strains from the violins seemed to Dylan a fit background for Janet Cloud's bereavement. He watched sorrow cast its hard shadow over her eyes; sorrow for a man who probably cared for little else during his lifetime but satisfying his own appetites. But sorrow had still found a quiet home in her heart. Dylan felt strangely saddened at Breaux's ability to continue bringing pain into her life, even from the grave. He continued, "At least for the time being."

Janet composed herself, the lines and contours of her face forming a pleasant mask. She swallowed the last of her tea and stood up. "I have something that may be of some help to you. Come with me."

Dylan got up and followed her down a dark hallway to the back of her house. She entered a small room off the porch and switched on the light. A closed venetian blind covered the single window. A straight-backed chair sat at an oak desk with a green-shaded banker's lamp and an old Royal typewriter. Several black-and-white prints of jet fighters — soaring against backgrounds of massive cumulonimbus and delicate, wispy cirrus cloud formations — hung on the walls.

On the desk, a mother-of-pearl frame embraced a more personal print. A young and dashing Dickie Breaux, circa 1952, stood on the tarmac of an air base in Korea next to an F-86 Sabre jet. He wore a flight suit, a brilliant smile, and gave the impression of a stocky Errol Flynn.

Janet opened a closet door, pulled the string on a ceiling light, and lifted a cardboard Trappey's Black-Eyed Peas carton down from a shelf. Tied with heavy twine, it bore the words *Dickie's Things* scrawled in red crayon. She carried the box to the desk and set it down. "Dickie's mother gave this to me the day he was killed. Said she couldn't bear them in the house any longer."

"He was living with her, wasn't he?"

"There, more than any place else, I guess."

Dylan untied the twine and opened the box. He smelled the perfume scent first, then glanced down at a clutter of letters and photographs, mostly of young, attractive females. Quickly closing the box, he turned to Janet. "I'll take these down to the office if you don't mind. From the looks of it, we're in for a long haul, running down all these possibilities."

Janet merely nodded and left the room, stopping at the door. "Turn the light out will you?"

Dylan could hear her heels clicking on the hardwood floor. He picked up the box, turned out the light, and followed her back down the hall.

"I appreciate your help," Dylan said as Janet opened the front door for him. He glanced at the box. "Don't say anything about what's in here, will you?"

"Sealed." Janet touched her lips with two

fingers. "I promise."

Dylan saw a curtain of sorrow drop across Janet Cloud's face as the door closed with a clicking of the lock.

3

Every Honeysuckle Blossom

Dylan parked Emile's white Blazer in front of the courthouse in Clinton, a little hill-country town north of Baton Rouge. Massive white columns formed a lofty portico on all four sides of the building. An example of classic Greek Revival architecture, it dated from 1841 and was the oldest active court-house in the state. A lone Confederate sol-dier looked down from his high pedestal set among the live oaks.

Live oaks and white columns. Dylan glanced around the quiet little town with its grocery, dry goods, and hardware stores and a two-pump filling station. *No wonder Hollywood used this place for so many movies. It's almost like a parody of the South.* He remembered when *The Long Hot Summer* was filmed and how the "Varner" signs had remained tacked on the front of town businesses for months after the movie had been completed.

Dylan grabbed a dark brown corduroy

jacket from the seat next to him and got out of the Blazer. He wore a white dress shirt, freshly ironed Levi's, and brown loafers. Climbing low stone steps, he took the brick walkway past the soldier to the courthouse, then pulled open one of the heavy double doors of the south entrance and entered a dim lobby.

Twin staircases climbed the left wall with a door between them that led out to the sheriff's office. At the north end of the lobby another door opened onto "Lawyers Row," with buildings as old as the courthouse. To the right of this door sat a Coke machine and stacked wooden cases, some holding empty bottles. Dylan slipped his jacket on and crossed the lobby.

Dropping a quarter into the slot, Dylan opened the machine's narrow glass door and pulled out a ten-ounce bottle of Coke. He popped the top off in the built-in opener and sat down on an empty case, killing time, putting off the thing that brought him to the courthouse today.

"What brings you this far north, Dylan?" Billie Ashford, bubbly and bright, wore her "going to court" outfit, a tailored charcoal-colored suit and white silk blouse. Her shiny-clean brown hair was shoulder length with bangs hanging straight down above her scrubbed face and Colgate smile. "I thought you'd found Shangri-La down there in Evangeline."

Dylan kissed Billie on the cheek as she placed one hand on his shoulder and leaned toward him. "I'm here for something I have absolutely no business at all doing," he told her.

"Sounds like you haven't changed a bit then."

Taking a swallow of Coke, Dylan exhaled slowly. "Why do they always taste better out of bottles?"

Billie knew he didn't expect an answer. "C'mon. Why'd you come up here?"

"I know you, Billie. You'd just laugh at me."

"No, I won't." Billie raised her hand holding two fingers up, "Girl Scout promise."

"You heard about . . ." Dylan stared at his bottle of Coke, "Dickie Breaux and the mayor of Pierre Part?"

"Who hasn't?"

"Well, the governor got together a task force representing the law enforcement agencies in the area, and Emile sent me to represent our department." Dylan watched Billie fight to keep the corners of her mouth from turning up.

"You?" Billie's eyes grew even brighter

with amazement. "On a governor's task force!"

"That's right," Dylan admitted, regretting now that he had mentioned it. "We met in Baton Rouge for two days, and now I'm supposed to train the sheriff's department here to protect their mayor from assassination."

Billie slapped her hand over her mouth, but the laughter slipped around the edges of her fingers, then burst through completely.

"Girl Scout promise, my foot! I knew you'd laugh," Dylan chided.

People entering and leaving the courthouse had begun to stare in their direction. Billie took deep breaths and finally managed to control her laughter. "I have a confession," she grinned. "I was never even in the Girl Scouts, Dylan."

For some reason this sent Billie into another fit of laughter. Dylan settled down on his Coke case, merely shrugging when people stared and pointed toward Billie.

Billie stopped, brushed her eyes dry with her knuckles, and gazed at Dylan. "I kept remembering our days together in the good ol' Welfare Department when we always made fun of task forces and other such bureaucratic nonsense."

"I didn't have any choice, Billie."

60

"Sureee," Billie said slowly, skeptically. "My friend Dylan, the company man."

"Now that you've had enough laughs for a month or so, how about giving me a little information."

"What kind?"

"The kind I called you about last week when I found out I was coming up here."

Billie glanced around as though someone might overhear what she was saying. "I did a little research — or as you'd probably call it, investigation. First of all, the newspaper's story was inaccurate."

"Imagine that."

"There was only one child in the custody of the Welfare Department missing . . . not five." Billie illustrated with her fingers. "And . . . there were only two missing from the Juvenile Department, not three."

"Anthony White's brother, Jerome, your foster care boy, and Remy and Russel Bastiste from the JD."

"Right. The official departmental policy is 'hands off.' " She leaned closer to Dylan, lowering her voice. "Our cases have been turned over to the proper authorities, and we're to terminate any further action on them."

"Proper authorities?"

Billie's voice became barely audible.

"FBI. At least that's the rumor."

"Sounds like the powers that be in state government are overreacting a bit. A person might tend to think they're trying to cover up something."

A shadow flickered across Billie's bright eyes. "I'm sorry, Dylan. That's all I could find out."

"Well, our cases on Remy and Russel are still open. Everywhere I turn I hit a stone wall, but sooner or later something's going to lead me in the right direction."

A lingering sadness touched Billie's face as she spoke. "I miss those days when we worked together, Dylan."

"We had a few laughs, didn't we?"

"And then there were times when we stopped laughing." Billie glanced at the sudden brightness as the door across the lobby opened. A chunky man wearing a dark suit and carrying a briefcase walked quickly toward them, then turned right and disappeared down the hall. Her mouth softened as she turned toward Dylan. "That's what I remember most." She let her breath out slowly. "And now you're going to be a father."

"How'd you know?"

"The old civil service grapevine is still in good operating condition."

"Too bad the rest of our state government doesn't work that well."

Billie nodded. "Well, I've gotta run. I'm already five minutes late for an appointment." She clasped Dylan's hand briefly. "Come by for coffee next time you're up this way."

"Sure." Dylan watched her walk away, open the door across the lobby, then turn and wave, her hair nimbused by bright sunlight behind her. He remembered eight-year-old Anthony White on the day the judge had sentenced him to the Department of Corrections for stealing food. So thin his body looked as though it was made of chocolate covered sticks, he had clung to Billie. He wondered if his brother, Jerome, looked like that . . . and what had happened to him.

Dylan slumped on his wooden case, occasionally taking a swallow of Coke as he watched the citizens of Feliciana Parish go about their business. Jess Thompson walked over from the opposite stairwell where he had been blocked from Dylan's view by the upstairs landing.

Dylan nodded toward Jess and watched him come down the stairs toward him.

Thompson was of medium height and medium build, but the .44 magnum slung low on his hip in a western-style holster was an extra large. His eyes were the color of pine bark, their steely glint reminding Dylan of his DI in marine boot camp. Light from the high window glanced off the front of his scalp beneath thinning brown hair. He wore mahogany-colored cowboy boots and a tan uniform.

Thompson walked over to the Coke machine, nodded at Dylan as he selected a Coke, popped the top, and took a long pull. "They always taste better out of bottles," Thompson said, his back toward Dylan.

"You going on a rhinoceros hunt?" Dylan asked, eyeing the .44 on Thompson's hip. "Looks like that thing would wear you out, packing it around all day."

"You get used to it. Matter of fact, I walk a little kankered to the left without it," Thompson said as he turned and grinned, bending from the waist to illustrate for Dylan. "They can keep them nine-millimeter jobs. This is more accurate, got more stoppin' power, and —" he patted his holster twice, "if I get a misfire, it don't shut down on me like an automatic would."

"I take it the answer to my question, after that short history of American handguns, is *no*."

Thompson let the remark pass, then

looped his thumbs through the top of his gun belt. "I hear you come up here to teach us how to stop that madman from killing our mayor."

Dylan held his stare, knowing he was going to face the same kind of harassment from the other deputies. "This wasn't my doing, Jess."

"I wouldn't think so," Thompson said. His chin wrinkled, his bottom lip pushed at the top, and a deep chuckle burst from his mouth. "Sorry." He took a white handkerchief from his back pocket and wiped his eyes. "I just can't see you teaching us how to do that."

"I can't, either," Dylan agreed quickly. "I'd be happy to have you take over."

Thompson held his hands up in protest. "No sir, not me. You got this duty."

Dylan swallowed the last of his lukewarm Coke, knowing Thompson would soon finish his session of throwing verbal spears.

"After all, you been a deputy for . . ." he paused, "how long is it, two months?"

"Just about."

"That oughta make you an expert, all right." Thompson's eyes narrowed as he turned them on Dylan. " 'Course you did make it over to Nam. Marines, right?"

Dylan nodded.

"See any action?"

The scene came rushing back in spite of Dylan's attempts to block it out. *The roar and scream of the helicopter's engine as the pilot revved it up for lift-off; elephant grass flattening in the downdraft; AK-47 slugs spanging off the airframe; the big blades throp-thropping. . . .*

"Not much."

"Well, you must have run across some tough customers in parole work," Thompson conceded. "I reckon that counts for something."

"If you say so, Jess." Dylan dropped his Coke bottle into a slot in the case next to him. "Look, the governor's got to rattle his saber a little. That's what this is all about. The task force is a political show to let voters know he's right on top of this assassination business, whether it does any good or not." He stood up. "But it wouldn't hurt to listen anyway. Common-sense things like having somebody with the mayor all the time, at work, home; wherever he is."

"I don't think that's gonna work," Thompson argued. "Mayor likes his private time too much."

"Maybe he doesn't have to know about it. Just have somebody keep an eye on him."

Thompson smiled lazily. "This is a quiet little town, Dylan. The last murder we had was six years ago. You really think there's any danger?"

"My yes!" Jimmy Iverson, the mayor, broke into the conversation. "Danger lurking behind every magnolia tree and every honeysuckle blossom." His sandy hair was parted precisely and slicked down on his round head, and his fair complexion was reddened already by the May sunshine. He wore a blue seersucker suit, white shirt, frayed slightly at the collar, and a canary yellow tie. Only ten pounds overweight, his five-six frame and his pie-shaped face made it look like more. "Yessiree, this is a mighty dangerous town, Dylan. A regular hotbed of cold-blooded psychopaths and colder-blooded assassins."

"Morning, Mayor," Thompson said, grinning at the little man's tirade. "I was just telling St. John here that he needn't worry about anything happening to you."

The corners of the mayor's light blue eyes twinkled with good humor. "Well, I think that's absolutely true," he agreed, "as long as I stay out of the local juke-joints and out of bedrooms I got no business being in."

Iverson, smiling sweetly at Dylan, tugged at his collar with a forefinger. "I'm ever so grateful for your interest in my safety, Dylan, but I *do* believe your time could be used more effectively elsewhere. The assassin type just doesn't bloom well here in Feliciana Parish."

"That's right," Thompson agreed. "We weed that type out early and ship them on down to New Orleans." He gave the mayor a conspiratorial glance. "By the way, that's where you're from, ain't it Dylan . . . New Orleans? Now, that's where you oughta be lookin' for your killer."

Dylan ignored their remarks, accepting the fact that when two men cut from the same cloth — like Iverson and Thompson — got together, it was pointless to try to retaliate. He knew full well he wasn't in their league when it came to mindless blather. "Whoever's doing this isn't normal — and he's not likely a local," Dylan explained. "It looks like some kind of vendetta."

"Maybe he's just plain crazy," Jess offered. "I hear there's a lot of that going around these days."

"That too," Dylan agreed. "But he's smart; good planning, no clues, and no motive we can find."

The mayor pulled an almost-clean handkerchief out of his back pocket and mopped his damp forehead. "There's lots more pleasant ways to spend a spring morning in Feliciana, Dylan, but I guess you must do what you must do. As for me, I have pressing

68

business over at the barber shop." He bade them good morning and swung away down the hall, his crepe-soled shoes swishing on the polished tile floor.

Dylan listened to the sound of Iverson's whistling as he vanished through the bright doorway. "Well, he's always pretty cheerful, but I don't think I've ever seen him that happy. He's almost giddy."

"Been that way for two or three days now," Jess mused, stroking his chin with thumb and forefinger. "Only times I've ever seen Jimmy this happy is when you sit him down in front of a big banana split. Maybe he's . . . nah."

"What're you talking about?"

"Nothing. Let's go." Thompson turned and headed toward the door between the staircases that led out to the sheriff's office. He called over his shoulder, "I know all the boys are sitting on the edge of their seats, waiting for you to get there."

Dylan pulled the Blazer into the tin-roofed shed that stood on a narrow strip of land between the road and the water. Cutting the ignition, he listened to the ticking sounds of the engine cooling down and breathed in the smells of damp earth and musty old timbers. Through the doorway that opened to the water, he watched a snowy egret spread its wings and lift slowly away from the top of a piling that supported the dock. The late sun, dropping behind the treeline on the opposite bank, cast most of the bayou's surface into deep shadow.

Dylan let his eyes wander around the gloomy interior of the shed. An aluminum bateau hung from the ceiling joists; a ten-horse Mercury outboard was screwed down tightly to a two-by-four nailed to the wall. Hunting and fishing gear hung from nails and cluttered the shelves. He remembered a night less than a year before when he had sheltered here while a howling storm raged outside and hidden by the night and the wind and the rain drumming on the roof, an assassin had stalked him.

Getting out of the Blazer, Dylan walked out onto the dock, its planking weathered to a silvery gray. He sat down in an aluminum chair with nylon webbing and propped his feet up on the piling the egret had flown from.

"Dylan —"

He glanced over his shoulder toward the board-and-batten cabin. Susan stood in the doorway, barefoot, wearing a pale yellow sleeveless dress. Her hair was still damp from the shower and her face scrubbed clean, shining in the shadow of the cabin's gallery facing the bayou.

"It's me all right." He motioned for her to join him. "The hunter home from the hill."

Susan walked the length of the gallery and crossed a two-by-twelve that connected it with the dock. Pulling a chair over next to Dylan, she leaned over, placed her hand against his cheek, and kissed him soundly on the lips. "What news has my hunter brought back to the swamps?" she asked, sitting down.

Dylan gazed into his wife's eyes, the color of hard mint candy beneath its frosty sugar coating. "The news is . . . there *is* no news. How about the home front?"

Closing her eyes, Susan leaned her head on the back of her chair, her voice like a sighing breeze. "I just love it down here." She slowly opened her eyes, gazing at the lengthening shadows on the far side of the bayou. "Sure had my doubts though. A New Orleans girl stuck out in the swamps away from shopping centers and street lights and beauty shops."

"And traffic jams and air pollution and street thugs that would gladly cut your throat for the price of a cheap bottle of wine," Dylan amplified her analogy.

Susan took a deep breath, letting it out slowly. "Even if the city didn't have all those

71

things, I'd still like it better out here." She sat up, her eyes intent on Dylan. "You mean you didn't find out anything at all today?"

"I found out that the deputies up in Feliciana don't take kindly to outsiders telling them how they ought to do their jobs." Dylan unsnapped the holster holding his .38 Smith and Wesson revolver, slipped it off his belt, and laid it carefully on the deck planking.

"I thought the governor wanted that done as part of his task force."

"They knew that," he grinned, thinking of the surly, or restless, or merely bored expressions on the faces of the men he had faced only hours before. "Didn't seem to make much of an impression on them though."

"No news about Remy?"

"Well, I did get a little break there. Billie told me there was only one child missing from the custody of the Welfare Department. . . . Not five like the newspapers said. Him and Remy and Russel Bastiste from the JD."

"Billie . . . who's Billie?"

"You remember her. We used to work together at the Welfare Department." Dylan watched two tiny vertical lines form between Susan's brows and knew then that she did remember.

"She's the one," Susan's eyes narrowed as

she glanced at Dylan, "that left her husband and started looking for another one the next day. I do remember her now."

"Well, anyway, *that* was good news. I don't know if we'll ever find any of them, but I don't plan to give up. I'll have to put this assassination business ahead of it for now though." Changing the subject, Dylan smiled at Susan and asked, "How's my Wimbeldon champ getting along today?"

Susan instinctively placed the flat of her hand across her stomach. "He's resting nicely, thanks." The creases above her brow flickered briefly. "You know there's always the possibility *he* could be a *she*."

"I've noticed there's another sex, Susan," Dylan said with a somber expression, "and I have to tell you that I approve heartily of the arrangement."

Susan smiled. "You wouldn't be disappointed if we have a girl, then?"

"If she looks like you, I'll take two any day."

Susan stood up, then slid down onto Dylan's lap as he straightened up in his chair. "I'm so happy now. I hope things go on like this forever." She leaned sideways against him, resting her head in the hollow of his shoulder.

Dylan laced his fingers around her waist

as he remarked lazily, "You really like it down here, huh?"

"Hmmm. Life seems so much slower. There's time to enjoy things like sitting on the bayou with your husband and watching the sky turn lavender and pink, and seeing the stars twinkling in the sky when it reaches that midnight-blue stage. I love the nights here on the water and the sounds coming from way off in the swamp."

"And you don't miss the big city?"

"It's less than an hour away, even from down here next to the Basin — and Emma goes in almost every week, so it's a nice trip and a chance to visit with her." Unbuttoning his shirt, Susan let her fingertips trail across Dylan's chest as she spoke. "In the summertime when I was a little girl, Mama and Daddy used to take me to their camp down in Lafitte. We'd stay there two or three weeks at a time, and sometimes Daddy would have to go all the way back to New Orleans two or three times a week to take care of things at the office, but Mama and I would stay at our little cabin on the lake even when he'd have to stay in the city overnight."

Dylan smelled the clean, flower-fresh scent of Susan's skin; felt the caress of her hair against his cheek. He knew that he would never understand how the sound of her voice and the touch and the fragrance of her seemed to siphon away all the knife-edged uncertainties of his day.

"We'd fish and swim and pick blackberries, and Mama would make the best pies I ever tasted." Susan's voice had grown softer than the sound of the evening breeze rustling through the reeds growing at the edge of the bayou. "I remember I used to tell her I wished all the days were summer so we'd never have to go back to the city."

"You never mentioned that your folks had a camp before. Do they still use it?"

"No. Daddy sold it when I was nine. He just got so busy he didn't have time to go there anymore."

Dylan glanced across the bayou at the shadowy palmettos standing in fanlike profusion at the edge of the forest. The water was darkening, picking up a slight tinge of the lavender sky. Listening to Susan's words of faraway times and places, he felt the touch of her fingertips idly trailing their warm paths across his chest; felt the soft yet firm reassuring weight of her body against him, and accepted the fact that he didn't deserve such happiness as this.

After a silence, Susan said, "This little house here on the bayou reminds me of that place and those times."

Sliding his left hand up her back, Dylan stroked her damp hair, cradled the side of her face, turning it upward toward his. "Thy lips are like a thread of scarlet . . ."

Susan sat up in his lap, a question mark in the center of her face. "Are you all right?"

". . . and thy speech is comely."

"Oh, the game," Susan said with a nod of her head, realizing she was to guess either the poet or the poem or both. "Shakespeare? Yes, that's from the ol' bard's pen."

Shaking his head, Dylan continued, "Thy lips, O my spouse, drop as the honeycomb . . ."

"The Bible . . . it's from the Bible, isn't it?" Susan asked, turning her face toward him.

Dylan nodded. "Honey and milk are under thy tongue . . ."

Susan clapped her hands against his shoulders. "Song of Solomon!"

"I applaud you."

"I didn't know you memorized Bible verses."

"I don't — usually," Dylan admitted. Grasping Susan's wrists, he kissed the palms of both hands. "You don't have a grandfather who's a preacher without learning a little Scripture though. I remember spending time with them in the summer." His eyes stared at something in the deep purple sky just above the treeline. "We had a Bible study every evening."

Susan took his face in both hands, kissing him warmly on the mouth, then slipped away and headed across the two-by-twelve walkway that led to the gallery. "Supper's ready in fifteen minutes."

Dylan watched her walk away toward the little cottage, thinking of something he had heard years before. He couldn't remember who said it, but the words had remained with him. *What world deserves attention more than this?* It was a question that no longer needed asking. This was his world now, and he made up his mind that moment on that twilight bayou to give it all the attention it deserved.

4

The Tie Pin

The Feliciana Courthouse on that mild May night resembled a dream of the Antebellum South. Bathed in pale moonlight, the white columns rose in lofty elegance, forming a shining colonnade around the old building, constructed twenty years before the shelling of Fort Sumter.

Hollis Henry, the night marshall, loved the courthouse and found in it a comforting friend as he patrolled the quiet town. He dreamed of the Old South and Shiloh and the wearing of Confederate gray, and of the hooped-and-parasoled women that would surely have swooned as he galloped past them, his saber flashing in the sunlight.

Someone — nobody could remember who — had once compared Henry to a particularly stringy piece of beef jerky made from an old, old cow. Much to Henry's chagrin the name *Jerky* had stuck, and after decades of carrying it around with him, he had never quite grown accustomed to its constant chafing. He stood five-seven and — wearing his thick-soled engineer boots and khaki uniform, complete with the big gold and blue-enameled badge he had designed and paid for himself — weighed one hundred eighteen pounds.

At 1:53 A.M. Henry sauntered along Main Street, his foul-smelling cigar blunting the scent of the gardenias growing in front of the brand-new Feliciana Bank and Trust building, complete with columns, in miniature impersonation of the courthouse. Sitting down on a brick ledge that bordered the bank steps, he gazed across the street at the old courthouse. "Right purty," he said around the soggy cigar clenched between his teeth.

Henry took the stub of cigar out, flicked it into the street, and picked a strand of tobacco from between his yellow teeth. Glancing around, he continued his nightly monologue. "I jes' don't understand it. Ever woman I run across treats me like I'm a polecat at the town flower show. I know I ain't no sprang chicken, but fifty-seven ain't that *old*, neither."

Noticing movement across the street, Henry squinted and held his hand above his eyes against a non-existent sun. Even at that distance, Henry kept his voice low, never openly using his pet name for the man who signed his paycheck. "Looks like ol' 'Lardbucket' Iverson's had too much to drank agin."

Henry stood up and adjusted the Sam Browne that held his .38 revolver, his eyes still fixed across the street on the dim figure, leaning for balance on one of the massive columns. "Even 'Lardbucket' over there got married. I wouldn't have that mousy little wife of his," he muttered, "but look at *me*, I can't even get myself *one* date."

A bell tower in a nearby church bonged the hour of two. Creeping around a corner of the bank building, a scruffy cat the color of diesel exhaust eyed Henry and melted back into the shadows.

"Guess I better get back on my rounds. Iverson's so sloshed he probably won't remember a thang tomorrow — but you jes' never know. Catch a man sittin' down one time and — zap — he's out of a job." Henry, his eyes still turned on his boss, noticed a faint red glittering. "Mighty fancy tie pin he's got there. Guess Miss Mousy bought it for him for being such a perfect husband."

Across the street, the mayor lurched away from the column, slowly raising his left hand in front of him.

Henry smiled, waved at the mayor, and

sauntered off around the corner, his heavy boots thudding against the sidewalk, impersonating the sound a burley man would make. The screech of a frightened cat and the clanging of a garbage can lid broke the stillness of the night. "Shoot! You stupid cat — tryin' to scare me to death!"

In the moonlit colonnade, Iverson stood with his left hand slowly clawing at the scented air in front of him, his gaze fixed in disbelief on the red jeweled hilt of the dagger protruding from the center of his yellow tie. Suddenly he dropped to his knees and slumped over on his right side, his dull blue eyes staring beyond the spot where Henry had stood watching, beyond the quiet town, out into the empty, endless dark.

Humming along Highway 10, Jess Thompson kept his speed under eighty . . . barely. Dylan sat next to him in the dark blue Ford with its two-way radio on the console, a twelve-gauge pump shotgun clamped beneath the dash, nightstick, mace, and other accessories of civil warfare cluttering the seat and floorboard.

Dylan wore a khaki shirt, new Levi's, and cowboy boots that Emile had insisted he buy because all the other deputies wore them. Dylan's small victory in the matter had been buying a pair with low heels and slightly rounded toes.

Glancing at the Feliciana Forensic Unit off to his right behind its high fence, Dylan pondered the sometimes contradictory workings of the legal system. The staff combined their efforts toward trying to make prisoners sane enough to stand trial, then spend their time in prison or be strapped into an electric chair and zapped with 10,000 volts of current. From what he had learned, any of the three alternatives was preferable to staying in Forensic where chemical restraints had replaced whips and chains, meaning each prisoner was administered a quantity of Haldol sufficient to sedate a musk ox.

Dylan turned back to Thompson. "You sure this little journey is about Iverson's murder?"

"Yep." Thompson wheeled south onto Highway 68, the Ford's tires protesting with a muted screech on the blacktop. "Wanted to get away from the office. I don't want any of them ol' boys spreading rumors around town."

Knowing that the deputy would eventually reveal his reason for asking Dylan to meet him on his own time, Dylan contented himself with staring out the window at Dixon, a medium-security state prison. Across the rolling pasture beyond two high fences topped with razor wire, men in denim trousers and light blue shirts worked out with weights, or stood, or sat, or walked in groups or by themselves, each wishing he was somewhere, anywhere else.

Minutes later Jess slowed down and pulled into the parking lot of Asphodel Plantation. "We're gonna meet somebody here," he announced. "It's out of the way," he said and grinned at Dylan, "and besides, they got the best praline cheesecake this side of New Orleans."

Dylan thought of how much Iverson, lying beneath the red clay soil of Feliciana for one full day now, had liked cheesecake. *Strange, the things you remember about people.*

Thompson found a parking place between a sweet gum and a cedar that looked as though it had been standing in 1820 when the house was built. He glanced at three charter buses parked at the end of the gravel lot and observed, "Gonna be crowded today." Opening his door, he glanced at Dylan, and barked, "What you waitin' on?"

"If you're not interested in broadcasting this meeting, why such a public place?"

"I told you, it's off the beaten path, and if somebody *does* see us, they won't suspect

83

anything out of the ordinary in a place so obvious." Thompson blew his breath out between his lips. "Look, I'm just doing this to protect Iverson's wife and family from gettin' hurt by something that might not even be true. This place does a big night-time business, but for lunch it's mostly retired folks or a couple up from the city for a special treat . . . not much chance of seeing anybody locked into the Feliciana grapevine."

"Whatever you say, Deputy. This is *your* party." Dylan opened his door and stepped outside, walking with Thompson toward the main entrance located on the wide front porch. He had passed the place many times but never given it a good look. Doric columns forming the central gallery and two flanking wings provided the main features of the fourteen-room house. The grounds held guest cottages; a train station, circa 1900; and a large Louisiana colonial townhouse where the restaurant was located.

Inside, the elderly vacationers from the buses occupied most of the tables, filling the air with their sharp Ohio consonants. Dylan waited patiently while Thompson spoke with a skinny man in overalls. Then they made their way across the smooth pine floor to a table that looked out onto a park-like area in the rear.

As Dylan pulled out a chair, he glanced around the home-turned-restaurant with its high ceilings, heavy beams, and paneled and papered walls. Even the pale, yellow-gold light that filled the room looked old, like scraps of sunshine left over from a hundred summers.

The waitress headed across the dining room toward their table, rubber-soled shoes squeaking on the polished floor. Her hair was dyed the approximate color of the red plastic nametag that identified her as *Mavis*. She had a blunt face with a pug nose and a fat little mouth. "Hey, Jess, how you doin'?" Mavis asked brightly.

"Good, Mavis. How 'bout you?"

"I'll do in a pinch." She held her yellow pencil poised above a ticket pad. "Who's your friend?"

"This is Dylan. Dylan — Mavis."

"Oh, like *Bob Dylan!* I just love him, especially that song *Rainy Day Women*. That's what Sammy, he's my boyfriend, calls me; his rainy day woman. One time —"

"Mavis, can we order now?"

Mavis tilted her painted eyebrows in Thompson's direction. "Certainly!" she huffed. "It's gonna take a while though, with that bunch off the buses."

"Three of whatever today's special is. That

all right with you, Dylan?"

Dylan merely shrugged.

Mavis used her stubby forefinger to point. "One, two — where's the third one?"

"Just bring us the food." Thompson glanced over his shoulder toward the front door. "He'll be here."

As Mavis stomped off toward the kitchen, the front door eased inward, letting in new light with the old. Hollis Henry, straw cowboy hat cocked on his narrow head, stepped inside, looking the place over.

Thompson took a quick look, then turned toward Dylan, slowly shaking his head. "I told him not to wear that stupid uniform. He's got a head like a fence post."

Spotting Thompson, Henry strolled deliberately across the room toward him, turning his head slowly from side to side, his eyes narrowed in concentration as though expecting an ambush from behind one of the linen-dressed tables. He pulled out a chair, sitting with his back to the window.

"I told you not to wear that uniform, Jerky! It just attracts attention."

Henry flinched at the sound of his nickname. His heavy badge tugged his shirt downward toward his trousers. Polishing it with the back of his sleeve, he said, "This is official business. I aim to dress official, and what's more . . . "

While Henry lectured Thompson on the finer points of law enforcement protocol, Dylan gazed through the tinted window at a fox squirrel climbing to the upper limbs of a hickory tree.

". . . and besides, the women jes' *love* a man in uniform. You never know when the right one's gonna bump into you." Henry finished his brief exposition and folded his arms across his narrow chest.

"You finished?"

"Yep." Henry strained his neck toward the kitchen. "Something smells good. What we eatin'?"

"Whatever the special is," Thompson said flatly. "Now let's get down to business."

"That's what I come fer," Henry said, grinning at Dylan.

"Anything you can tell us might help," Dylan explained. "We're taking everything we learn and sending it to the Baton Rouge headquarters. They're trying to piece it all together, kind of like making a big quilt. Eventually the pieces might lead us to the killer."

"A big quilt, huh?" Henry seemed to be having difficulty with the analogy.

"Well —" Thompson had obviously begun to lose patience. "St. John here is on the governor's task force, and he didn't come up here to watch you shine your badge."

Henry stopped the rubbing motion of his sleeve, then placing both elbows on the table, locked his hands together. "Okay. Here it is then." He gave one furtive glance around the room before he began. "Last week, Thursday night I thank it was, I seen ol' Lar —" Henry stopped himself and began once more. "I seen the mayor coming out of his office about one o'clock. And he wudn't by hisself, neither. No sireee Bob."

"Could you just give us the facts, Jerky?"

Henry scowled at Thompson, but continued. "He had hisself a woman. Good-looking, too, from the little I could see of her."

"Could you give us a description?" Dylan took a small note pad from his shirt pocket, placed it on the table, and clicked a white ballpoint pen.

"Kind of a little gal — five-two, maybe three — slim build, but not skinny, if you know what I mean. Purty long dark hair, mighta been black, couldn't tell for sure . . . too dark."

Dylan finished his notes and looked up at Henry. "You ever see this woman before?"

"No sir." Henry showed his yellow teeth. "I'd shore remember a gal like that if I had."

"Anything else?"

88

"That's about it."

Clicking his pen closed, Dylan put it and the note pad back inside his pocket. "Iverson never seemed like the type to do this kind of thing, Jess."

"Never known him to before," Thompson said, rubbing the back of his neck, "but then I guess every man can have his weak moments."

"How long you been working nights, Officer Henry?"

Henry's face brightened; he sat up a little straighter in his chair. "Eleven years. Ol' Lar — I mean, the mayor, appointed me right after he took office."

"You ever see him out with any other women?"

"Never," Henry said flatly. "He never run around as far as I know — not until now anyway. I can't understand what he saw in that little wife of his, but —" He stopped in mid-sentence as though something had clicked inside his head. "Hmmm, I wonder if she'd want to —"

"It's way too early for that, Jerky," Thompson interrupted him. "Her husband was buried *yesterday*."

Henry grinned sheepishly. "Yeah, I know. I oughta be ashamed of myself, but still —"

Thompson glanced in the direction of the

kitchen. "Here comes our food. You finished, Dylan?"

Dylan nodded, staring at Henry's face. His yellow teeth were still bared in the smile he had forgotten to remove, and his eyes had taken on a faraway look.

Far above Capitol Lake, fluffy white clouds drifted against a sky as blue as a summer sea. Across from the towering seat of government, Our Lady of the Lake Hospital sat on the bluff rising from the lake's mirrored surface. Hydrangeas brightened the entrance with their deep blue color while lavender four-o'clocks scented the air for visitors as though making amends for the neon glare and antiseptic smells they would surely face inside.

Dylan pulled the Blazer between the white stripes of a parking space in the lower lot near the lake and hurried up the two levels of steps into the lobby. A sturdy, middle-aged woman wearing a white uniform and a dour expression sat at the front desk.

"Susan St. John's room, please," Dylan said. Something about the woman looked familiar.

She frowned over her reading glasses as she glanced up at him and asked, "Are you a relative?"

Dylan thought he recognized her then. Six months before, he had been sliced above the eye by a parolee who had preferred his freedom over returning to jail. She had been on duty at that early morning hour when he had been brought to the hospital. "Didn't you used to work in the emergency room?" he queried.

"Do you always answer a question with a question, young man?"

"Yep, it's you all right," Dylan said aloud, realizing he should have kept his thoughts to himself.

"Are you trying to cause trouble?" Her voice lowered to a raspy growl. "If you are, I'm sure one of the security guards will be happy to accommodate you."

Dylan cleared his throat. "No ma'am. And yes, I am a relative. I'm her husband."

"Poor thing." She ran her finger down a lined page, then gave him an over-the-glasses scowl. "Room 253."

Smiling his thanks, Dylan turned and headed toward the elevators. After the doors swished open on the second floor, he stepped out into the hall. The smells of floor wax and that ineffable odor of sickness followed him down to room 253.

Gently pushing the door open, he saw Susan's pale face in the shadowy room, her

91

dark hair spread on the white pillowcase. He eased over to the side of the bed, its chrome railings gleaming in the murky light.

"Dylan —" Her voice sounded almost childlike in the still of the room. "How did you get here so quickly? I thought you'd gone up to Feliciana."

The room had the hushed quality of a small chapel. "Emile got me on the radio just after I left for Evangeline."

"Glad you could make it." She smiled weakly and held out her hand.

Dylan leaned over, kissing her on the forehead and taking her cool hand in his. "Are you all right?" *Stupid question! If she was all right she wouldn't be in a hospital.* "Emile knew you'd been taken up here and that's about all."

"Sure," Susan said, slipping her free hand over his. "Just a little spotting. The doctor wants to keep me overnight to make sure everything's okay."

"I'll stay with you."

Susan shook her head. "No, sweetheart. That's not necessary. You can take me home tomorrow. I'll call you as soon as the doctor comes by to see me."

"You won't have to do that."

"Why?"

Dylan pulled a chair over next to Susan.

Sitting down, he took his shoes off and propped his feet on the bed. " 'Cause I'll be right here when he comes."

Susan smiled, her head turned toward him. "But you're working on this thing about the mayors' getting killed. That's important, isn't it?"

What world deserves more attention than this? Again the words came back to him. He thought of the trifling, uncaring disuse he had once made of his wedding vows, letting Susan gradually slip away from him. *Never again!*

"Not as important as you." Dylan knew she had already relented, but still felt obliged to lodge this final mild protest. "Besides, there's dozens of people working on these murders, but only *one* who's having our baby."

Susan closed her eyes and said softly, "It's nice knowing you're here with me."

The afternoon light through the blinds cast a pattern of thin gold bars and shadows across the bed. Staring at Susan, Dylan watched her breathing, slow and regular and saw her face relax as sleep took her on a journey he could not share. He noticed her Bible next to the water pitcher. She kept it near her most of the time now and seemed to draw strength from its words, written so long ago. Then he felt his own eyelids grow heavy, letting his head find the back of the chair. He yawned deeply and drifted away.

He sprinted through the rice paddy, his jungle boots kicking up mud and water. Breath ragged, chest heaving, he clutched his M-16 in both hands and leaped over the dike just as a mortar round hit behind him. Shrapnel whistled like mad hornets overhead as he landed hard on the other side, grunted in pain, scrabbled around like an animal in its lair, and pressed in hard against the damp earth of the bank.

"You can really haul it when you want to." Corporal Vince Cannelli, a stocky, curly-haired baker from Queens, lay on his back, his helmet pulled low over his forehead, a Camel dangling from his lips. He and Dylan had been close friends since boot camp.

Dylan, inspecting his weapon to see that it was not fouled by mud, gulped air into his burning lungs. "Next time you take the point, Cannelli."

"I'm a better shot than you are," Cannelli said through the blue-white smoke drifting upward in front of his face. "That's why the lieutenant keeps me back for covering fire. Besides, I can't run as fast as you."

"Maybe that's because you're not as scared as I am."

Cannelli laughed in spite of the fear glazing his eyes.

In the stifling heat, sweat poured from Dylan's body, burning his eyes, soaking his fatigues. He mopped at his face with a soiled green handkerchief. His breath rasped in his dry throat. Unscrewing the top of his canteen, he let the last few ounces of tepid water pour into his mouth, swished it around, and swallowed.

Machine gun rounds from the edge of the thick jungle clipped away at the top of the dike, trying to eat their way through it to the marines it protected. Three more mortar rounds exploded almost simultaneously, sending showers of black earth and one green-clad body hurtling through the air. A jagged piece of shrapnel whanged off the side of Dylan's helmet.

"They'll be coming now." Cannelli tried to control his speech, but a note of hysteria had crept in. He slammed a full clip into his 16, took a deep breath, then turned his dark eyes on Dylan. "Time to rock and roll, buddy."

"Uhhh . . ." Dylan jerked his head up, the dream still running in his mind. Gradually the scenes faded; he heard Susan's voice.

"Dylan . . . Dylan are you all right?"

"Hmmm . . ." Rubbing the sleep from his eyes, he sat up in the chair. "Yeah, sure. I just had this kind of strange dream."

"About what?"

"Well," he began, running a hand through his hair, "I dreamed I was awake, but when I woke up I was asleep."

Susan was silent for a moment, then she smiled. She patted the mattress. "Come over here next to me."

Dylan stood up and then sat beside her on the bed.

"I mean really next to me." She turned on her side, her back toward him.

He stretched out carefully, slipping his left arm beneath the pillow. Then embracing her with his right arm, he felt her take his hand in both of hers, pressing it close. "You sure the nurses won't mind this?" he whispered.

"Shhh!"

Dylan embraced that same comforting warmth he had always felt with Susan next to him. Her hand on his was better than any pill, better than any therapy dreamed up by the soothsayers in their white coats or tweed jackets. He thought briefly of a darkness deeper than the night; a darkness created in a lethal and tormented mind, and of the killer who lived in that dark. But all that could wait until tomorrow. For now, there was only *this* world where the troubles of his day seemed as remote and insubstantial as a fable.

PART TWO

Shadows

5

The Rooster and the Fox

Emile must have looked like that at his age,
Dylan thought as he stared at the color print
of the young soldier, a bright smile on his
lean, tanned face, his newly issued uniform
as sharp as a recruiting poster's. Turning the
picture frame around to its original position
on the desk, he leaned back in a brown
leather chair studded with brass and watched
Emile walk through the door of his office
carrying two thick white mugs of coffee.

"Good picture of Robert," Dylan commented. He nodded toward the desk as he
took the offered cup.

Sitting down in his squeaky oak swivel
chair, Emile glanced at the photograph and
said, "Yeah. Brought it in this morning." He
took a sip of the steaming coffee. "I looked
just about like that when I was nineteen."

A silence crept into the office after the brief
conversation about Robert. Outside the open
window, a mockingbird trilled from the slick

branch of a crepe myrtle. Slow traffic droned along the street. Dylan watched Emile's eyes, drawn back to the picture, take on a remote quality; then Emile busied himself with the coffee. Dylan glanced about the office: green filing cabinets on one wall, three drawers not quite closed; a map of Louisiana from the Department of Highways on the wall behind Emile next to a detailed map of Maurepas Parish.

"Susan all right?" Emile asked finally.

"Yeah. I brought her home this morning."

Emile paused for a moment. "Can't be a jealous husband."

At the abrupt change of subject, Dylan thought about the meaning of Emile's words, then spoke. "Not much doubt about that. Unless his wife's got a thing for small-town mayors."

"And he's got nothing to do with his time but follow her around and take his revenge," Emile finished the thought. "Whoever this guy is, he gives me the creeps."

"Not as much as he does the mayors of the little towns around here, I'll bet." Dylan remembered the last time he had seen Jimmy Iverson: jolly, joking, harmless. *Why would anybody want to kill a man like that?*

Emile got up and went over to the chalkboard next to the Maurepas Parish map.

Four columns were scrawled in his handwriting. *Victims, Method, Motive,* and the last, *KILLER,* in bold block letters. He took a piece of chalk and tapped it next to the first column. "Now what do we know about the victims?"

"All mayors of small South Louisiana towns," Dylan said as Emile wrote.

"Two were involved with at least one woman other than their wives — except for our own Dickie Breaux, who'd run around with so many women before and after his divorce it'd be hard to put a number on it."

"Anything else?" Emile asked. Holding his chalk next to the green board, he glanced at Dylan.

"That's all I can think of."

"Method," Emile said, writing *medieval weapons* beneath the column heading. "All handmade as far as we can tell — the first case with the sword threw us for a while because the murderer didn't leave the weapon, and we didn't have any kind of pattern. So it was probably some kind of broadsword. The boys at the State Police Crime Lab struck out, and there's no way I can think of to trace the dagger or the crossbow bolt."

"Motive," Dylan repeated, as Emile

moved to the next column. *"Hates politicians."*

"That narrows it down to about two million suspects," Emile said as he tossed the chalk from one hand to the other. "Does he hate politicians in general, or mayors to be specific? That's what we need to know."

"Maybe he just doesn't like men who cheat on their wives," Dylan remarked. He tried to put himself in the mind of someone who could carry around that much cold, calculating rage. "A bad marriage of his own . . . unfaithful wife. Could be the dark side of honor, fidelity — thinks he's been appointed as some kind of knight errant to right the wrongs of the world."

"Sounds a little bizarre to me," Emile said, holding Dylan's gaze.

"As bizarre as these murders."

Emile nodded slowly, his eyes narrowed, then began scratching with the chalk. "You're right." When he finished, he underlined the word *KILLER* with a harsh stroke of the chalk.

"He's small, slim, and a good athlete," Dylan said, thinking of the lithe, dark figure he had seen bounding off the oak limb, sprinting through the light-splashed shadows to the blue Chevy on the day Dickie Breaux was killed. "And a pretty good driver."

"*Proficient with medieval weapons,*" Emile added, lengthening the list.

Dylan stood up and walked over to the board. "I think he's pretty well off financially, too. He's spent so much time planning, practicing, and plotting, I don't see how he could hold down a regular job."

Emile nodded as he wrote. "*Intelligent.* Not much doubt about that. Didn't leave any clues at all — except the ones he left on purpose."

Scanning the four columns, Dylan thought of how the killer had backtracked and lost them somewhere along the winding road across the Mississippi. "He didn't seem to have any trouble getting away from us, either."

"I'm not so sure that takes a whole lot of intelligence," Emile said, his face expressionless.

Dylan gave him a wry smile. "Now, where does all this deduction lead us?"

Tossing the chalk with a flick of his wrist, Emile caught it without looking as he studied the board. "Looks like it takes *us* right down a blind alley." He gave Dylan an oblique glance and dumped the chalk on the board's narrow ledge. "But it leads *you* out into the Basin."

"The Basin?"

"You know — that big swamp with all the cypress trees and water."

Ignoring the sarcasm, Dylan went back to the desk and plopped down on its edge, sipping his coffee.

Emile sat in his swivel chair, creaking it slowly back and forth. "Muskrat Verrett came to see me yesterday." He leaned forward, elbows on the chair arms, eyes strained from the brightness of the window behind Dylan. "He's a trapper, hunter, and fisherman born in the Basin — lived there all his life. Says there's been some strange goings on out there."

"That's a strange place," Dylan agreed as he pictured moss-draped cypress towering above the eerie stillness of dark water, where twelve-foot alligators slipped beneath duckweed covering the surface.

"He said he found a place that looks like some kind of training ground."

"Training — for what?"

"That's exactly why you're going out to Muskrat's cabin — to find out."

"That Basin's a mighty big place, Emile. I'm more at home with the hills and pine trees of Feliciana where I used to spend my summers." Dylan glanced out the window. "You sure I can find my way around back in there?"

"It's time we found out." Emile pulled a map out of the middle drawer of the desk, unfolding it on top of the desktop clutter. "I've got it marked right here."

Standing up, Dylan stepped next to Emile and leaned on the desk with both hands.

"This is where you and Susan live. Now all you have to do is follow the lakes and bayous and pipeline canals along this red line, and you can't miss it."

Dylan stared down at the maze of converging lines on the map. "You want me to use that bateau and the ten-horse Merc in the shed?"

"Unless you'd rather swim."

"Well, I guess if I'm going to work down here, I've got to learn the Basin sooner or later."

Emile traced the twists and turns of the waterways with his finger. "Right here. He lives in a tin-roofed shack with a rose garden in front."

"A rose garden?"

"Yep. Muskrat loves roses." Emile began refolding the map. "Roses and bubble gum." Reaching into a bottom drawer, he pulled out a carton of Fleer's Double Bubble gum and dropped it on the desk. "Give this to him. You'll make a friend for life."

"Is this man sane, Emile?"

"You tell me after you meet him."

Dead limbs, decaying leaves, and ragged, black husks littered the ground beneath a hickory tree rising from the hammock of land that Muskrat Verrett had chosen for his home. Mushrooms, buttercups, and blue bonnets sprang from the dark soil. The underbrush had been cut away long ago, leaving only the tall, widely-spaced trees, their limbs and trunks wrapped and hung with thick vines.

Dylan cut the engine, letting the flat-bottomed bateau drift across the dark water toward the clapboard shack. It was set back from the edge of the small lake in the deep shade of two ancient tupelo trees. Concrete-block steps led up to a gallery that held two straight-backed chairs with deer-hide seats.

Out front in an open space beneath the cloudless blue sky, roses bloomed in shades of red, yellow, and peach. A single bush in the center of Verrett's garden spilled over with white blossoms. A gasoline generator's muted growling broke the stillness of the morning.

As the bateau slid up onto the muddy bank next to a battered handmade pirogue, Dylan stepped out and pulled it halfway out of the water. He wore an old pair of Converse tennis shoes that had once been white, sun-faded Levi's, and a pale blue T-shirt. The carton of Double Bubble was cradled beneath his arm. Cupping his hand to his mouth, Dylan called out, "Anybody home?" The steady drone of the generator from somewhere behind the shack was the only reply.

Dylan walked through the rose-scented yard toward the front porch along an old path leading through the new and verdant growth of spring weeds. The porch creaked when he stepped onto it. The sound of piano music playing on a scratchy record drifted through the partially opened front door.

Knocking on the door, Dylan glanced at the mud-caked and battered brogans that sat just to the right of the door. He thought of the work shoes his father had always placed at the back door of the home he had grown up in. The music made an elegant counterpoint against the racket of the generator's engine. "Anybody home?"

The music stopped. A chair scraped. Dylan listened to the faint creaking of the house as someone inside moved toward the front porch. The door swung slowly away from him, revealing the house's dim interior, streaked with slats of sunlight.

"Something I can do for you?"

Dylan stared at the narrow face and slim nose that almost came to a point above thin lips and amazingly white, straight teeth. Neatly parted down the middle, his thick white hair still held stubbornly on to a few brown streaks. A red flannel shirt and threadbare overalls hung limply on his spare frame.

"My name's Dylan St. John with the Maurepas Sheriff's Office. Emile DeJean said you might have something to tell me about some unusual happenings out here."

The man held out his hard brown hand. "Alton Verrett. People call me Muskrat." He glanced down at the carton of bubble gum in Dylan's hand.

"Here, this is yours. Emile sent it."

Verrett showed his white teeth, took the gum, and turned back inside the house. "Come on in," he called over his shoulder, "and make yourself at home."

Dylan stepped into the dimly lighted, warm interior. A black cast-iron stove sat in the far corner of the one-room shack, a box of split wood on the bare floor beside it. Against the wall next to a curtainless window sat a handmade table and two ladder-back chairs. Several shelves held a meager assortment of dishes, canned goods, sugar, coffee, flour, and other staples. A single iron bunk with a thin mattress covered by a green army blanket stood against the opposite wall. The smell of old grease and tobacco smoke permeated the room.

"Have a seat," Verrett offered. He dropped the bubble gum on the table, pulled out a chair, and sat down.

Dylan noticed the old RCA record player at the head of the bunk. It sat on a wooden spool that had once held telephone wire and now served as a nightstand. "That was a nice piece of music playing when I stepped up on your porch."

"Chopin," Verrett said, opening the carton of gum. "One of his piano concertos. I forget which one. The machine plays the old 78 rpm records. Kinda scratchy." A smile spread across his veined face as he gazed at his treasure of gum.

Dylan watched the old man unwrap two pieces of gum and plop them into his mouth, then begin to read the funnies on the wax paper wrappers. He found himself uneasy in the presence of this solitary man who seemed perfectly content with only himself for company.

"Can't buy the 78s anymore, so I have to be careful with the ones I have."

Dylan glanced around the interior at the stacks and shelves and boxes of books: the classics, mysteries, reference books, hardback and paperback, as well as a dozen or so Bibles. He asked, "Did you read all these books?" realizing that it was a silly question before he had finished speaking.

Verrett turned his faded brown eyes on Dylan. "Now, that's a silly question." He chewed with obvious relish as he spoke. " 'Course I have. Most of 'em two or three times. You got any books you don't want, why just bring 'em on out here. I'll see to it that they get a real good home."

"I usually keep my books," Dylan answered, feeling more comfortable now that he had found some common ground with the little man who was now furiously blowing bubbles. "I like to read them more than once, especially the poetry."

Verrett turned his old eyes, now holding a more youthful light, on Dylan. "You actually read poetry?"

Dylan nodded. "I've even been known to write it on occasion. There might be some who'd argue the point, but I like to call what I write poetry."

"A young man who works for the sheriff's office, but still finds time to write poetry." Verrett seemed to speak to no one in particular. "Maybe there's some hope out there after all." He used the words *out there* as if he were describing a world other than his

110

own. Blowing a huge bubble, he popped it with his tongue, drawing the gum back into his mouth.

Dylan had begun to find Verrett an incongruous and fascinating figure. "You mind if I ask you a few questions?"

Pop! The gum disappeared back inside Muskrat's mouth. "Not a bit. Ask away."

"Why do you stay out here all by yourself?"

Verrett chewed thoughtfully. "I tried living in town — once. Lasted six months." *Pop!*

"What happened?"

"Married a girl I knew from high school right after I got back from France."

"France?"

"Yep. I fought the dreaded Hun in World War I. How's *that* for a quick lyric?" Verrett's smile gave him a boyish appearance in spite of the lines and sags of age. "Poison gas; living in muddy trenches with rats the size of small dogs for roommates; holding my best buddy down while a French doctor worked on him — no morphine, nothing to kill the pain." His eyes held a remote light as he spoke. "That little episode over there tended to sour me on my fellow man." *Pop!*

"What happened to your wife?"

"I couldn't stand living in town, and she lasted exactly two weeks out here in the Basin," Verrett said as he looped his thumbs in

111

the straps of his overalls and leaned back in his chair. "She got married again and had three children. Somebody told me she died about three years ago."

Dylan had almost forgotten why he had come to see Verrett. "What's so bad about living in town?"

"The barbarians are at the gates, young Dylan."

Somehow Dylan knew it was the only answer he would get from Verrett. His mind turned back to the reason for his trip out into the Basin. "Maybe you could tell me something about the . . . unusual goings on out here."

"Better than that. I'll *show* you." Verrett stood abruptly and headed for the back door.

Dylan followed him out onto the back porch, cluttered with trapping and fishing gear. The generator rattled away on its two-by-four stand.

Verrett stepped over to it, flicked a switch, and it died with a wheeze followed by a groan. He gazed down a path leading into the deep woods that began twenty yards from the porch. "We got a thirty minute walk. You in shape?"

"Fair."

"We'll find out."

★ ★ ★

Slogging and splashing across a narrow bayou behind Verrett, Dylan drew the warm humid air deeply into his lungs. Striated light, the color of the buttercups in Verrett's yard, filtered down through the towering green canopy. The path had long since given way to thick tangles of underbrush and vines, sloughs, and whining clouds of mosquitoes. Dylan slapped one, leaving a black and red paste against the side of his neck.

"This is it," Verrett announced. He walked ahead a few paces, then crouched against the base of a sycamore tree, its trunk the size of a Volkswagen. Verrett signaled for quiet, then motioned Dylan to join him.

Beyond the old man, Dylan saw a brightening in the wall of shadowy green and knew they had reached a clearing. He moved silently over to Verrett, placed his hand on the old man's shoulder, and knelt next to him on a carpet of moldy leaves.

Pushing back the limb of a fledging magnolia, Dylan peered out into a meadowlike area the shape of a rough oval about fifty yards across and a hundred long. The only sound he heard other than his own labored breathing was the cawing of a solitary crow ringing across the stillness of the swamps.

"C'mon. Nobody's around." Verrett stood

up and stepped out into the clearing. "I haven't heard anybody back here for about two weeks now."

Dylan followed him out into the opening. Near the treeline on the far end, an assortment of rectangular-shaped plywood boards had been nailed to the trunks of several large trees. They walked across the clearing to take a closer look. Verrett ran his hand over the splintered wood that had been pierced in hundreds of places.

"This is where they practiced with the crossbows," Verrett explained. He pointed to the opposite end of the clearing. "They stood right over there."

A pipeline canal bordered the lower end of the clearing. The hulls of flat-bottomed boats had left shallow grooves in the bank. On the opposite side, a half dozen creosote poles stood upright about eight feet apart. Crude effigies, made from men's suits complete with neckties and stuffed with pieces of cardboard and old rags, had been bound to the posts with grass ropes. They were ripped and hacked to shreds and pieces.

Verrett walked next to Dylan. "And that's where they practiced with their swords and daggers and maces."

Dylan felt a chill working its way up his spine. "Did you see who did this?"

"Yep." Verrett's gaze turned inward as though recalling the scenes he had witnessed in the clearing. "Eight of 'em. Six men and two women. Wore armor and helmets. Looked like Camelot come to life out here."

"Think you could recognize any of them if you saw them again?"

"I doubt it. My eyesight's not what it used to be." Verrett studied the mutilated effigies. "Besides, I didn't want to get too close to that bunch."

"I've got to get somebody from the State Police Crime Lab out here. See if they can come up with anything."

"I doubt they will."

Dylan didn't bother to ask Verrett why. For some reason he felt the same way. He also suspected that their names were more likely to turn up on the social register than on a police report. "You may be right. We haven't had any luck so far with the two murder weapons we've got."

"People like that got too much time on their hands. Too much time and too much money." Verrett's thin brown finger traced a deep groove in the post next to him. It had been made by a vicious slash with an edged weapon. "They usually end up in one kind of mischief or another."

Dylan considered the horrors that Verrett

115

had faced in World War I that caused him to apply the word *mischief* to the possible involvement of these people in three murders.

Verrett's body seemed to sag within the baggy overalls. "I managed to get away from this kind of thing for a long time, but now they're bringing it out here to me in the Basin." He sat down and leaned back against a post, drawing his knees up. "I've lived seventy years in this old world, and I just can't figure out why man is so bent on hurtin' his own kind."

Dylan sat down next to Verrett on the soft ground. "These people may not be involved in anything illegal, Mr. Verrett. It could be just a way of letting off steam; just some kind of longing for the past . . . like *Miniver Cheevy*." For some reason he felt a little embarrassed, mentioning the obscure poem by Edwin Arlington Robinson.

Verrett's face brightened as he turned toward Dylan. "You know Robinson's work?"

"A little."

" 'He missed the medieval grace of iron clothing.' I was always fond of that line." A bemused smile lingered on Verrett's face as he spoke. "I sometimes think I was born too late — just like ol' Miniver Cheevy."

Dylan thought of all the years Verrett had

spent alone in the isolation of the trackless Atchafalaya Basin, and of the disappointment or perhaps despair he had found in the company of other men and women that had driven him there. "Maybe you've got a lot in common with these people. They seem to be as interested in the old ways as you are."

"Yeah." Verrett gave a short hollow laugh. "About as much in common as a rooster and a fox."

"I don't understand," Dylan admitted, puzzled as to why he thought Verrett fascinating. Yet he found that he couldn't quite keep up with the twists and turns that the old man's mind took.

"They both have a genuine interest in the henhouse," Verrett said, a hint of irony in his voice, "but entirely different plans for the chickens."

Dylan stared at the torn effigies and realized that Verrett was absolutely right. This introspective and gentle man could have very little in common with the violence evidenced in this medieval training ground.

"Think this'll help you any?"

Dylan shrugged. "Looks to me like all it does is complicate things. We thought we were looking for one murderer, now we may have at least eight possible suspects."

"The longer I live the less sense the things

people do makes to me."

"We thought at first it might be a jealous husband or boyfriend," Dylan confided. He spoke out loud as if to try to untangle his own thoughts about the cases. He knew he shouldn't be discussing them with Verrett, but he also knew that the old man would keep his own counsel. "Now with three murders in three different parishes, that theory doesn't hold up."

Verrett's voice sounded laden with weariness as he spoke. "I read a little bit about it in the newspaper when I went in for groceries two or three days ago. If you ask me, you're right about one thing."

"What's that?"

"It's only one person — and it's somebody that thinks the law can't touch him." Verrett stood up, leaned over, and rubbed his thighs with both hands. "I expect he's used to getting away with just about everything he wants to."

Dylan felt it was time to stop thinking about the case for awhile, so his thoughts could sift down to the bottom of his mind and perhaps sort themselves into some kind of logical order. He stared out at the pipeline canal, sunlight winking on the water's dark surface, the far shore in black shade. "If it wasn't for my wife, I might just join you out

here." Glancing at Verrett, he continued.
" 'Course I'd have to live a mile or two away.
Wouldn't want things getting too crowded."

Verrett smiled at him, but his eyes held a
lingering mist of sadness. "You're a man
after my own heart, young Dylan."

6

Susan of the Swamps

"What do you think about Muskrat?" Emile, straight from court in his tan suit and deep red tie, added a liberal portion of Louisiana hot sauce to his po'boy. Made with fresh-baked French bread — brown and flakey outside, soft and white inside — it was piled high with crusty fried oysters on a bed of lettuce and sliced tomatoes and so thick he could hardly get his mouth around it to take that first big bite.

"I think he's an intelligent, thoughtful man," Dylan answered. He glanced around the quiet interior of Paw-Paw's Cafe, located in an old bank building directly across the street from the courthouse. Red-and-white checked tablecloths and framed color prints of swamp scenes, local festivals, and historic landmarks brightened the dimly lighted dining area. With the lunch hour rush over, they shared the place with one other customer, a chunky man nursing a cup of coffee at the counter. He wore a tan raincoat, green slacks, and black oxfords. "The name Muskrat doesn't suit him at all."

Emile chewed slowly, enjoying his succulent and spicy lunch. "He got it when he was a boy. You know how a nickname sticks around long after anybody remembers how it ever came about in the first place."

"He's got some interesting ideas about what's happening to this country," Dylan said after swallowing his first bite. He was beginning to think the food in Evangeline would almost be reason enough to live there. "I might go back once in a while — not on business, just to visit."

"I figured you'd like him. Y'all have a love of casual dress in common, for one thing."

Dylan glanced down at his faded Levi's and tennis shoes still carrying smears and chunks of swamp mud. "Guess I should have stopped by the house and changed."

"I guess you'll do for Evangeline." Emile gazed out the window at the scattering of people walking beneath live oaks on the courthouse grounds. Changing the subject, he said, "So we may have eight suspects now instead of one. The more I find out about this case, the less I know."

"Verrett still thinks it's just one person," Dylan told Emile. He recounted his conversation with the old man out at the clearing deep in the Basin. "I believe he's right."

Emile took another bite, chewed thoughtfully, and swallowed. "It's the only thing that makes sense."

"You get in touch with the State Police?"

Glancing at the courthouse clock, Emile said, "They ought to be there about now."

Dylan fished an object out of his shirt pocket and dropped it on the table. "I dug this thing out of a board they used for target practice."

Emile examined the wedge-shaped shard of metal. "Arrowhead. Probably from a crossbow bolt."

"It's made of iron, not steel." Dylan watched the man in the tan coat reach over the counter, take the coffee pot from its warmer and pour himself another cup. "Just like the sword and the dagger. This is important to him for some reason."

Dylan found that he had lost his taste for food. "What do we do now?"

"More legwork. We haven't run down all the members of Dickie's harem yet." Emile gave the man at the counter a look of appraisal. "Still got a ways to go on checking for any leads on the east bank where he got off the ferry."

"I thought I might run down to Bridge

122

City in the morning and look through their records. See if I can find anything that might help us find Remy and Russel."

Emile nodded.

"You think our buddies over at the FBI might get territorial about that?"

Turning his eyes toward Dylan, Emile spoke in a hard flat voice. "Those boys lived in Maurapas Parish. I've known them since they were born."

It was the answer Dylan had been hoping for. "I should be back right after lunch." He wondered if any of the missing boys would ever be seen again.

Ding. Dylan turned toward the sound of the cash register drawer sliding open.

The chunky man in the tan raincoat stood behind the counter. His left hand reached into the money drawer, filling his pocket with bills. His right hand clutched a sawed-off twelve gauge, its stock cut down to form a pistol grip. The twin barrels swung slowly back and forth between Dylan and Emile.

"Take it easy with that thing, partner." Raising his hands, palms outward, Emile spoke in a calm, reassuring voice. "We don't want anybody getting hurt."

The man's pale eyes were glazed with fear and the amphetamine coursing through his veins. "Where'd the owner of this joint go?"

123

"To the bank."

"You better not lie to me!" The man had stuffed all the bills from the cash drawer into his coat pocket. "How'd he get out without me seeing him?"

"Back door," Emile said, pointing toward the kitchen area. "Leads out into the alley."

The man scooped most of the coins out of their slots, the shotgun weaving around in his hand. "I'm going out that way. Either one of you moves . . . he's a dead man."

"Door's locked."

"You're lying."

"Try it." Emile nodded toward the back entrance directly through the swinging doors that led into the kitchen area.

"Just sit right where you are and put your hands on the table." The man stepped sideways to the kitchen entrance, then glanced over his shoulder. Swinging the doors inward until their hinges locked them open, he backed slowly to the entrance that led into the alley. All the while he held the shotgun on Emile and Dylan, trying to steady its motion with his left hand. Reaching behind him, he tried to turn the door knob, jerked frantically on it, then muttering a curse, returned to the dining area.

"I'm going out that front door." His left eye had begun twitching. "If one of you moves a muscle," he took a quick look over his shoulder, "he loses his head."

Dylan knew that Emile would never allow the robber to reach the street and courthouse area where someone could be seriously wounded or killed. The fact that the man holding the shotgun didn't know they were cops gave them a slight edge on whatever they tried to do.

His movement hidden by the tablecloth and the downward angle of the man's vision, Dylan eased his left foot up slowly toward the seat of the chair that fronted the man's path. Resting the sole of his tennis shoe lightly on the chair's front edge, he readied himself by easing his right hand slowly toward the windowsill.

The man continued to walk stiffly toward them. In the crowded confines of the narrow room, he had to pass directly between their table and another only four feet away. Distracted, he bumped into the back of a chair, making a scraping noise on the bare concrete floor. Instinctively his finger tightened on the trigger, then eased up.

The black, round holes of the shotgun barrels looked as big as sewer pipe as they weaved closer and closer. Dylan could see the dark stubble on the man's sweating face. Thick eyebrows almost met above his short blunted nose. His breath wheezed through his distended nostrils. Glancing from Dylan back to Emile, he started the final fifteen feet to the front door.

"Just take it easy, son," Emile said. "Everything's going to be all right."

In his peripheral vision, Dylan could see Emile, relaxed and rock steady. An image of Susan, following behind a gurney down a hospital corridor flashed through Dylan's mind. In one swift motion, he braced his hand against the windowsill, kicked the edge of the chair seat as hard as he could with his left leg, and rolled onto the floor. The chair shot backward across the floor, thudding into the robber's legs.

Dylan heard a scream, the thunder of the shotgun and crashing of broken glass as buckshot shattered the window and splintered the table top where he had been sitting. As he came up on his hands and knees, he saw the barrels of the shotgun swinging away from him. Emile's right hand was beneath the left side of his jacket at waist level, his arm whipping around toward the man with the shotgun. A flash of fire erupted from the end of the .38's barrel, then a final roar from the shotgun.

Instantly the left side of Emile's white shirt sprouted red blossoms as the shotgun clattered to the floor five feet in front of Dylan's face. The man in the tan coat sprawled backward on the table behind him.

Dylan leaped from the floor to help Emile who was on his knees, the snub-nosed .38 still clenched in his right hand.

"Call Emmaline," Emile spoke between thin colorless lips. "Tell her I'm all right."

Dylan knelt beside him, holding him steady. "Lie down. I'll get some help."

Emile glanced at the shattered window. "Don't bother. They'll be here soon enough." He placed one hand on the table top. "Help me sit down. And don't forget to call Emma. I don't want her to hear about this on the radio."

Helping Emile into the chair, Dylan watched the man in the tan coat slide slowly off the table, crumpling in a lifeless heap onto the concrete floor.

Dylan pulled the Blazer into the shed next to the bayou. As he turned the engine off and sat in the gloom, weariness settled over him. Through the rolled-down window he breathed in the sharp, brassy smell of a storm moving across the swamp. Stepping out of the truck, he walked to the doorway and looked out across the water. Lightning flickered in the distance above the treeline, faint threads of white light webbing the sky.

Walking out onto the dock, Dylan sat down in the nylon-webbed aluminum chair. Thunder rumbled like artillery rounds out in the swamps. Directly across the bayou a great blue heron, the color of gunmetal in the shadowy twilight, stalked the shoreline for his elusive and finny supper.

Dylan could not push away the memory of the incident at the cafe. It kept jabbing at his mind like the sharp lethal beak of the heron. He had seen his own death in the robber's dark eyes and in their lifeless twins, the black empty relentless depths of the shotgun barrels.

The screen door of the little cottage squeaked open. Dylan turned and saw Susan carrying two tall glasses of iced tea toward the dock. It had become their custom to have coffee or iced tea together out on the dock when he got home from work early enough. Her slim legs looked almost luminous against the black shorts she wore as she walked toward him in the failing light. Her white peasant blouse was decorated with tiny ruffles and her dark hair fell in a soft, pleasing disarray about her pale shoulders.

Dylan felt again that same ineffable longing for her he had known when they first met, the same sweet aching in his heart. "It's my own 'Susan of the Swamps,' " he said, getting up and taking her in his arms.

"Be careful!" Susan warned as she held the glasses in outstretched arms to keep them from spilling over.

"Come live with me and be my love," Dylan whispered as he kissed her on both cheeks. "And we will all the pleasure prove."

Susan took a step back, handing Dylan one of the glasses. "That's easy — Christopher Marlowe."

Nodding, Dylan placed his hand along the clean line of her cheek, noticing the slight smudge of weariness beneath her eyes. "You feel all right?"

"Yep. I rested for a couple of hours this afternoon just like the doctor ordered. And I feel healthy as can be now." Susan glanced down at the weathered decking. When she looked up, her eyes were bright with tears. "Oh, Dylan!" Her voice trembled as she spoke. "You might have been killed!"

Dylan took the glass from her hand, setting it down on a small wooden table between the two chairs. Taking her in his arms, he caressed her hair as she stood on tiptoe, clinging to him, pressing her face against him. "Don't worry about it. It's all over now." He held her close, listened to the soft, trembling sobs, felt her hot tears against his neck.

Susan's voice was even softer than usual when she finally spoke. "Emile's wound wasn't serious?"

Dylan knew that Susan needed the reassurance of words, even though he had told her about Emile's injury when he had phoned her from the hospital. "Two of the pellets went through the fleshy part of his left side. The third one lodged near his hip bone. The doctor had it out in about five minutes."

"Emmaline's all right?"

"Perfect. She's spending the night with Emile." Dylan smiled, remembering his friend's face when he found out the doctor wanted to keep him overnight for observation. "He already had his clothes on to go home when she got there."

After an uneasy silence, Dylan said, "I could quit. Teach school or something."

Susan's troubled face relaxed, the corners of her mouth turning up slightly. "No, sweetheart. You wouldn't last a week shut up in a stuffy classroom."

Dylan pictured himself sitting in teacher's meetings, nodding off to the soporific voice of an administrator droning on about time studies or the latest budget crisis. "It might not be so bad," he said without a semblance of conviction in his voice.

This time Susan laughed out loud as she looked up at him. "I can see your future right now."

"What are you talking about?" Dylan said, his eyes meeting hers.

"I get this knock on the door in the middle of the day," she said, suppressing a giggle, "and there you'd be — standing between two burly men in white coats making your fashion statement in a conservative but stylish *straitjacket*."

"In khaki and denim, of course — my personal favorites." Dylan knew then that she would be all right. The fear would come back for a while, but each time it would grow weaker.

"We're going to ride in and visit with Emile and Emma after supper, aren't we?"

"Sure. They'd enjoy the company even if Emile is chomping at the bit to get out."

After holding her awhile longer, they sat side by side in the chairs, taking occasional sips of the cool iceless tea. The lavender afterglow had given way to night. A breeze swept through the tops of the trees and across the bayou, stirring its dark surface.

"I thought we'd catch that storm for sure," Dylan commented as he stared at the shining path of the moon stretching across the water.

"Guess it rained itself out before it could reach us."

Dylan finished his tea and pushed himself out of the chair. The two began to walk toward the cabin.

"What's for dessert?" Dylan asked out of the blue.

"Bananas Foster," she said.

"If I'd known moving down here was going to have this kind of effect on your cooking," Dylan said, feeling a glow of comfort inside him as he looked at their remote little cabin on the bayou, "I'd have done it years ago."

"And before dessert you get gumbo served with a baked sweet potato and cole slaw."

Dylan opened the screen door. "That's kind of an odd combination, isn't it?"

"An old Avoyelles Parish tradition," Susan explained. "I learned it from one of my sorority sisters at LSU."

"You'll have me weighing two hundred pounds by next Christmas."

Susan patted her stomach. "That's all right. You can just get fat right along with me . . . and the littlest St. John."

The Huey Long Bridge, completed in 1935, spanned the Mississippi just north of New Orleans. Located at the foot of the concrete and steel structure on the west bank,

Bridge City hosted the October Gumbo Festival — famous for its Creole gumbo, jambalaya, and oyster loaves. It was also year-round host to the Louisiana Training Institute, famous for burglars, purse snatchers, armed robbers, and other assorted underage felons.

Beneath the towering superstructure, Dylan hummed along the narrow roadway of the bridge in his blue '65 Volkswagen. The New Orleans skyline stretched to his left down river and beyond the city's other bridge. Dylan glanced below at a small sampling of the five thousand ships that annually visit the Port of New Orleans — the largest port in the world in water-borne tonnage — stretching seventeen miles along the river.

Sailing down the bridge's approach, Dylan entered the traffic circle on the west bank. Five minutes later, after showing his badge to the gate guard and placing a cardboard *Visitor* placard on his dashboard, he passed through the gate of the tall fence surrounding LTI and parked in a white-striped slot. Located in the shadow of the bridge in an area of industrial buildings, loading docks, and railroad spurs, the facility *allegedly* "trained" juvenile offenders to adapt to life outside of their *allegedly* controlled environment.

Dylan found Fred Nelson's office on the

second floor of the Administration Building. After accepting the mandatory cup of tarlike coffee in a chipped mug with the New Orleans Saint's emblem on its side, he sat down next to Nelson's desk in a metal chair with green upholstery. Noticing a tear in the chair's seat, Dylan tried to remember if he had ever been to a state agency that didn't have at least one green chair with a ripped seat in every office. *Maybe it's some kind of departmental policy.*

Nelson got down to business. "Here's what you asked for." He shoved a case file and a stack of sign-in sheets across the desk.

Dylan swallowed a sip of Nelson's coffee without making a face. He respected the stumpy little man with his gleaming Wildroot, slicked-down hair; his gray, ten-year-old J.C. Penney's suit; and the omnipresent scrap of toilet paper sticking to his neck where he invariably cut himself shaving. "You sure you won't get into trouble showing me this stuff?"

"No." Nelson had gone back to writing on a yellow legal pad with his nub of a pencil, glancing occasionally at an open case file, dog-eared and coffee-stained.

Opening the file marked *Batiste, Russel,* Dylan asked, "No you won't . . . or no you're not sure?"

"I'm *sure* all right," Nelson muttered into the legal pad. "Sure the powers that be will have my hide if they find out I gave those files to you."

Dylan stuck his ballpoint inside the breast pocket of his light blue sportcoat and closed the case record. "I'd better get out of here then. Thanks anyway."

Nelson reached across the desk, flipped the record open, and turned his flinty gaze on Dylan. "I want to find out what happened to Russel and his brother." He returned to his scribbling. "And right now it looks like you're the only hope I've got."

"What about the FBI?"

Nelson glanced up. "Weathervanes in suits and ties . . . and it doesn't take much wind to turn them . . . most of 'em." He tapped the point of his pencil on the desk. "There're a few good men in the Bureau, I guess. All stationed at Duluth or maybe Missoula, Montana."

"Thanks, Fred."

"Don't thank me. If you're serious, just get to work, or I'll put everything back in the filing cabinets."

Knowing he meant it, Dylan went to work. After two-and-a-half hours of poring over narratives, a plethora of forms, time sheets, and security records, he pushed the stack of papers aside and leaned back in his chair. "Tell me one more time what the gate guard and the cottage parent told you the night they took Russel."

Nelson gathered up a stack of yellow forms, tapped them on the desk to straighten them, and dropped them in a wire basket marked *Out*. "Two men in deputy's uniforms drove his mother, Rachel's her name I think, here in a sedan with MPSO decals on the doors. They arrived at the main gate at seven-thirty-seven, picked up Russel, and left at seven-fifty-three." He got up and walked to the coffee service behind Dylan. "But you already know all of that from the records."

"Just wanted to see if there was anything else you could add . . . something you might have forgotten about."

Pouring coffee into his mug, Nelson said, "I've gone over this a thousand times and can't find one thing we could use to run them down."

Suddenly Dylan's eyebrows raised, a look of astonishment on his face. "What's that?"

Nelson turned toward the framed poster on his left. "New Orleans' latest festival."

Dylan stared at the poster's image of a knight on his white charger, helmeted and armored, a gleaming lance in his hand. In the background, other knights as well as men garbed in rough peasant clothes fought mock battles with maces and broadswords. Others shot crossbows at targets. "How long has it been held?"

"First one was last year."

Dylan knew of Nelson's passion for South Louisiana festivals. Among the dozens of posters hanging on his walls, the Camelot Festival had almost gone unnoticed. "Tell me about it," Dylan said.

"I think some of the mayor's crowd, the ol' courthouse gang, started it. That's what I've heard anyway." Nelson returned to his desk, his face animated now as he discussed his favorite pastime. "Enamored as you are of things old, you'd probably like it. They recreate the days of Camelot; knights and maidens, lords and ladies. About four or five hundred people are supposed to dress this year from what I hear."

Four or five hundred more suspects, Dylan thought. *We'd better activate the National Guard.*

"Only about seventy-five to a hundred take part in the contests though."

"Contests?"

"Sure. They practice all year. Swords, lances, crossbows — the whole works."

What a break! Only a hundred more suspects.

"They use blunted weapons, of course,

and armor and heavy padding so that no one gets hurt."

Dylan thought of Evangeline's mayor clutching at the feathers in his throat. "No, we couldn't have anybody getting hurt."

Nelson shrugged as though he didn't understand Dylan's reaction.

"You mean you haven't heard?" Dylan said incredulously.

"Heard what?"

Dylan knew that the governor's office had tried to suppress the idea of a serial killer in the media. He also remembered Nelson's tendency to bury himself in his work, ignoring the media's propensity toward sensationalism. "Nothing important. When's this thing held?"

"Take a look."

Dylan got up and walked over to the poster. "That's this Saturday."

Nelson grinned. "You don't miss a thing do you? I'm surprised it's taken you so long to find those missing boys."

7

Patient Companions

Growing at the edge of the brick patio, a deep green gardenia bush spilled over with white blossoms, blending a heavy, sweet fragrance with the scent of roses. Palm fronds rattled against the stone wall in the breeze off the river and the calls of the neighbors still sounded as though all the residents of a street in Brooklyn had moved to Algiers, Louisiana.

Dylan slouched in a wrought-iron chair in the little garden behind his mother's house. He remembered the times before his father's death when the three of them would sit together while the day faded into dusk and the shadows of the tall, slate-roofed houses lengthened and covered the last scattered pools of sunlight. He had forgotten the words, their talk running to the small and unremarkable happenings that hold lives together, but the memory of those simple and trusting times had kept shining when other lights had gone out.

The screen door opened and Helen St. John stepped out onto the back porch. Wearing neat brown slacks and a tan cotton blouse, she cradled the heavy black telephone beneath her arm. Covering the mouthpiece of the phone with the palm of her hand, she asked Dylan, "You need to say anything else to Susan, dear?"

"No ma'am."

After telling her daughter-in-law goodbye, Helen set the telephone down on the porch next to her dead husband's scuffed brown work shoes, then joined her son on the garden patio.

Dylan stared at the shoes. They had been as much a part of his life as his red Western Flyer bicycle and his Red Ryder BB gun, and they had somehow made him feel safe when he came home from play and saw them next to the back door. "How long have those old things been there . . . fifteen years? Why don't you just throw them in the trash?"

Helen sat down in a chair next to her son. "You're a grown man now . . . you do it!"

Dylan smiled at his mother, thinking that she still knew him as well as when he was growing up in her house. "As clean as they are you must dust them off once in a while. Ever think about polishing them?"

Shaking her head, Helen answered, "No. They just wouldn't be the same all shiny and new looking. Noah had that brand new pair on when . . ."

"You're right. I like 'em better just like they are," Dylan said, feeling it was time to change the subject. "Think you're ready to become a grandmother?"

Helen's eyes held a grandmotherly light as she spoke. "I think I was ready when you were about fifteen." A shadow crossed her face. "Susan's not having any problems, is she?"

"Healthy as a horse."

"Good. I've been kind of worried about her." She reached over and patted Dylan's hand. "It's almost like old times having you spend the night with me."

"Yeah. I feel like I ought to be going on in to my room and working some algebra problems."

Helen gazed at her roses, their deep red color providing a pleasing contrast to the white gardenia blossoms. "You must have a nice boss to let you stay overnight like this."

"It's a whole lot better than a hotel room, and it saves the department money."

"Where did you say you're going tomorrow?"

"The Camelot Festival. It's out at City

141

Park." Dylan had decided long ago to let his mother know as little as possible about the nature of his law enforcement work. "There may be some people there who can give me information about a case I'm working on."

"Is it about those mayors that got killed?"

Trying to conceal his surprise, Dylan asked, "How'd you know about that?"

Helen glanced at her husband's shoes before she answered, a faint smile of remembrance lighting her face. "One of the reporters down here came up with the name, *The Camelot Killer*. I saw it in the afternoon newspaper." She turned toward her son. "Do you enjoy your work, son?"

Dylan realized that he hadn't considered work as something he should enjoy. "I never thought I'd end up being a cop, but it pays the bills."

"That's not much of an answer."

"Emile's a good man to work for . . . and I couldn't ask for a better friend," Dylan said and held his mother's gaze. "So I guess I'm better off than most people."

"And you and Susan seem to be getting along so well — and the baby's coming," Helen continued, "so I guess you have a lot to be thankful for."

As though a light had clicked on in the back of his mind, Dylan suddenly understood the nature of the worry he had brought into his mother's life over the past few years. "Maybe I'm growing up a little — you think?"

"Maybe so." Helen rose from her chair and walked over to the edge of the brick patio, where she knelt down and smelled one of her roses. Then she turned toward her son. "I think the beans are about done, and the sausage is already cooked. You ready for supper?"

"Yes ma'am," Dylan said, getting up from his chair. "It's been a long time since we had supper together."

Helen took his arm as they walked across the porch and into the kitchen. She glanced down at her husband's scuffed shoes, two patient companions calling back those days that now seemed like a pleasant dream.

The ax thudded into the target, its heavy blade slicing clear through the two-by-twelve pine board three inches to the right of dead center. Munching on a strawberry snow cone, Dylan leaned on the counter of a colorful red-and-white striped kiosk and stared at the man who had just thrown the ax. He wore soft deer-hide moccasins on his wide, flat feet, leather leggings, tight green trousers, and a brown floppy shirt. His white hair was cropped short above chiseled features and eyes that were almost colorless. Broad shoulders tapered to a narrow waist and thighs that bulged with muscle.

Man, I'd hate to tangle with that guy, Dylan thought. *He must be six-three, six-four; at least two hundred and twenty-five pounds.*

As though reading Dylan's mind, the big man turned in his direction, producing a smile that held no joy, no humor, and no good will. Dylan tried to remember if he had seen the man before. Then, glancing over his shoulder, he noticed that the white-haired man had in fact been looking beyond him at the next contestant, a chunky, bow-legged man walking behind Dylan toward the throwing area with his ax tossed casually against his shoulder.

Still, the smile that was not a smile caused a prickling sensation at the back of Dylan's neck. He watched the big man walk over to the target, jerk his ax free, and join the judge who was marking score sheets at a folding table.

Dylan found the Camelot Festival, situated among City Park's oaks near St. John's Bayou, a pleasant surprise. Amid the urban sprawl of New Orleans, it provided a recreation of the Middle Ages along with the modern conveniences of butane for cooking the gumbo, jambalaya, fried catfish and shrimp, hamburgers and hot dogs and french fries; electricity for cooling the drinks; and the ubiquitous and indispensable Porta-potties.

A realistic jousting match had pitted armor-clad, lance-bearing riders against each other on their sleek charging quarter horses. Dismounted by lances clashing against their shields, they had flailed each other with abandon, their heavy broadswords ringing off armor and metal helmets.

Chewing the sweet, red shaved ice of the snow cone, Dylan wandered the festival grounds among woodsmen with peaked green caps sporting tall feathers, ladies in long gowns and elaborate headdresses, and non-participants like himself clad in jeans and slacks, tennis shoes, and T-shirts. He watched a modestly clad Lady Godiva ride past on a champagne-colored palomino and wondered if she would have any affect on the city's tax structure.

Walking in the light-dappled shade of the live oaks, Dylan watched several archers readying for their shooting contest in a meadowlike clearing fenced off by blue-and-white engineer ribbons. Dressed in high leather boots, green tights, and loose-fitting brown shirts, they carried crossbows and wore belt quivers filled with turkey-feathered bolts. Seventy-five yards distant, at the far end of the sun-bright field, round, hay-filled targets with red bull's-eyes stood on tall wooden tripods.

This must be the finals for them to be shooting at such a long distance, Dylan thought as he sat down at the base of one of the massive trees. Resting elbows on knees, he studied the contestants, four men and one woman. The men were young and athletic-looking, exhibiting the casual confidence and easy manners born of country club locker rooms, manicured playing fields, lots and lots of leisure time . . . and money.

The woman blended in well with her fellows. Dylan thought that she must have been two or three inches taller than Susan, but with the wider shoulders and muscular legs of the weight room rather than the slim, feminine grace of ballrooms and bridge parties. Still, with the shining sweep of her dark hair falling below her shoulders, flawless olive complexion, and dark brown eyes, she presented a striking appearance.

The contest began and two men fell out of the running when the targets were moved to the ninety-yard mark. Only the girl and a blonde lifeguard-type remained when they were set at one hundred yards from the shooting line.

With one shot deciding the championship, the man stepped forward, released his arrow in one smooth motion, and then groaned when he saw the marker's signal from the target indicating that he had hit low and to the left.

Now it was the woman's turn. Tossing a single blade of grass into the air to test the wind, she placed her right foot an inch behind the chalk line and swung the bow up to her left shoulder. Making a final adjustment for windage, the woman released her arrow with a sharp snap of the crosspieces and a faint humming of the bowstring. Dylan watched the slim shaft climbing in a perfect arc against the blue sky, then take the downward curve of the parabola toward the bright circles of the faint, distant, improbable target. Dylan marveled at her skill and accuracy, as well as the craftsmanship of her bow. Constructed of a dark oiled wood, lightweight and amazingly strong, the bow sent the arrows straight and true.

An undertone of murmuring moved through the spectators as the marker walked across to the target, pulled the arrow free, and held his hand up in the signal that the shooter on line had almost, but not quite scored a bull's-eye. Bull's-eye or not, the woman's shot was enough to beat the competition.

She let out a yelp of victory, leaping and throwing her arms in the air as her fellow archers surrounded her, lifting her above their shoulders, chairing her through the select crowd that had gathered to watch. Someone lifted a magnum of champagne up to her. She drank liberally, drank again, then shook the bottle and sprayed her admirers with the frothy liquid.

Sitting quietly beneath the massive live oak, Dylan took in the celebration. In the course of the past few hours, he had seen a number of men and women proficient in the use of medieval weapons: the lance, broadsword, ax, dagger, mace, and now finally the crossbow. He believed at least one of them was capable of using his — or her — skill with antiquated weapons in the taking of a human life.

Dylan's thoughts turned toward the white-haired giant who had thrown his ax with such deadly accuracy and power. He focused his thoughts on the man's eyes. Carve out two chunks of a glacier formed in an ancient and violent time, add a bit of turquoise coloring and the glint of a steel sword; then bring them almost to life. Dylan shivered slightly in spite of the hot afternoon breeze.

★ ★ ★

"Did you enjoy my shooting?"

The slightly husky-sounding voice snatched Dylan from his thoughts. He gazed up into the face of the woman who had just proven herself the best crossbow marksman in New Orleans, maybe the entire South. The crossbow was slung over her back with a soft leather strap.

The first thing Dylan noticed about her was her arrogance; not blatant or coarse, but arrogance distilled to its essence. The second was health . . . glossy hair, glistening dark eyes, teeth so white and straight and perfectly formed they could have been made in a laboratory; perfectly clear complexion, glowing warmly in the hot June afternoon. He imagined that she would look exactly the same in a damp, cold December wind.

"Maybe you should audition for a Robin Hood movie," he suggested in reply. The fact that she had used the words *my shooting* and not *our shooting* or *the contest* was not lost on Dylan.

"Robin Hood used a longbow."

Dylan got to his feet and was surprised to find that the woman was no taller than Susan. "How *gauche* of me not to remember that! As I recall, only the villains used crossbows in merry ol' England."

The dark eyes sparked, then cooled instantly so that her anger went almost unnoticed. She turned her cool smile on Dylan. "Do you think I look villainous?"

"I think I don't know who you are," Dylan replied, seeing again the slim feathered shaft soaring against the sky before plunging to the target in a near perfect shot.

She held her hand out, as if she were greeting a new teammate on the college rowing team. "Dianna Salazar. My friends call me Sunny."

Taking the proffered hand, Dylan felt its coiled strength beneath the pampered soft skin. "Nice meeting you, Dianna. I'm —"

"Dylan St. John," she finished for him.

Dylan suddenly felt an icy tingling at the back of his neck; an old atavistic warning signal set off by something that his mind could not pin down. He thought that a mountain man a hundred years before may have felt something very similar when a vengeance-bent Comanche crept toward his camp, out of sight and making no more sound than a cloud passing over. Wrapped in the strange feeling, he couldn't seem to find any words in reply to the simple speaking of his own name.

"I went to college with you — at LSU," Dianna went on to explain as though speaking to an amnesiac. "I didn't really know you, but I did see you play a few tennis matches."

A sense of relief washed over Dylan, even though a cold mist still seemed to cloud his thoughts. "I . . . I don't think I remember you."

"That's all right," she responded. The smile remained, the moist lips curved nicely revealing white enamel, but the eyes remained watchful. "I was a year or two behind you, and I didn't really care that much for tennis anyway."

"Archery?" Dylan felt a sense of accomplishment in speaking the single, sensible word.

"How did you ever guess?"

As always, Dylan grew impatient with the thrust and parry of hidden agendas in chance meetings like these that had nothing to do with chance. "What's this all about, Dianna?"

Her laugh carried a raw edge of sensuality rather than humor. "Does it have to be *about* anything in particular?" She unslung her bow, leaned it against the tree, and sat down.

Dylan gazed at her upturned face. The signal was back, warning him to turn and walk away, but he knew somehow that the answer to unraveling the bizarre murders was inexorably bound to this not-quite-charming woman. "I find that most everything that happens *is* about something."

She laughed again, softer, the huskiness more suppressed. "Are you *always* so suspicious?"

"Usually."

"I simply recognized you and remembered what a good game of tennis you played — that's all. Not smart tennis, for you took too many chances and didn't play the percentage shots, but you had the natural gifts so you got away with it . . . most of the time." A thin sheen of perspiration covered her upper lip. She brushed it away with the back of her finger.

"I thought you didn't like tennis."

"I don't particularly, but I do appreciate seeing a good athlete, whatever sport he's playing." She seemed to be tiring of Dylan's interrogation. "It's awfully warm. Why don't you get us something to drink?"

Dylan held her gaze. "I'd rather have an answer to my question first."

Relenting with a sigh, Dianna continued. "My daddy gave you something once." Her eyes lighted with a secret mischief. "I was only about twelve or thirteen, but I still remember it," she said with a smile. "The courthouse steps. . . ."

Dylan blinked at the impact of her words.

152

Only once did he have occasion to receive anything on the courthouse steps. "Your daddy's Mayor Salazar?"

She nodded, her expression like that of a little girl revealing a playhouse secret. "I think the reason I remember is because he said something about your batting average and then handed you a tennis trophy. I thought it was funny."

Dylan smiled at the memory of that day that seemed like ages ago. Something about that simple shared moment of their childhood caused him to feel more at ease with Dianna. "So you're the mayor's daughter? I remember seeing your picture in the paper once or twice now, but it was a long time ago."

"I'm still thirsty," Dianna announced. Her patience had obviously faltered from the heat and Dylan's insistent questions.

Dylan marveled at the mercurial change in her disposition. He still heard the not-quite-hidden whine lingering at the end of her words. The childish pout on her lips reminded him of a six-year-old Shirley Temple, then it vanished. "Will a Coke do?"

"That would be marvelous!" she said. "And make sure there's plenty of ice."

Dylan nodded, wondering how he would ever learn anything from this unpredictable woman with her pampered past and troubling present.

Holding the red-and-white paper cups filled with ice and Coke, Dylan stared at the vacant spot where he had left Dianna. Gone also was the custom-made bow. A sudden movement out beyond the festival grounds caught his eye. She stood, arms akimbo, the crossbow slung across her back, her head and her disarming smile both tilted slightly to one side. Then with a beckoning, welcoming motion of her hand, she ran across the hard-packed ground toward a nearby lagoon with the agile grace of a wood nymph.

Dylan watched her move effortlessly among the shadows and the pale yellow light spinning down through the summer leaves of the giant oaks. Suddenly an image flashed in his mind; that slight, dark-clad figure leaping down from the low, spreading limb of the live oak, running swiftly, gracefully through light and shadow toward a blue Super Sport parked on the banks of Evangeline Bayou.

The thought had scratched at the back door of his mind as he watched the perfect curving flight of her arrow, but he had shut it out. Now he contemplated the unthinkable, trying to remain clear-headed and rational, believing that he had stumbled into the heart of darkness, hoping that he could find his way out.

Again he felt the almost overwhelming desire to turn and run away, but having had little practice at that, he walked deliberately into the shadows after Dianna Salazar.

"Over here," she called to Dylan.

Dylan saw her standing at the edge of the lagoon, its shimmering surface dimpled by red-eared bream feeding in the deepening twilight. He continued walking toward her, closing the distance between them. "I thought you'd gone home," he said as he reached the shoreline.

"I couldn't do that," she said simply. "I don't have a home to go to."

"Are you kidding?" Dylan handed her a paper cup of Coke. "I saw that place of yours in a magazine once. It's one of those mansions just off St. Charles Avenue."

Dianna spoke matter-of-factly, her voice as emotionless as though she had been called on to answer a question in history class. "It's a house."

Dylan followed her over to a stone bench at the water's edge and sat down three feet from her. She glanced at the empty space between them and smiled as though someone had just whispered a marvelous secret in her ear.

Across the lagoon the white-columned facade of the New Orleans Museum of Art stood like a piece of Athens set down in South Louisiana. A young couple, their voices soft across the water, floated past on a paddle boat.

"I used to come here sometimes when I wanted to be by myself," Dianna said softly as she gazed out at the wavering reflections of the white columns reaching toward them on the water's surface. "I had this adolescent fantasy that a lovely place would make you think lovely thoughts." She took a long swallow of her Coke, then added, "Too many movies, I guess."

"Maybe just too much free time."

The eyes sparked again, then her laughter washed them clear. "You don't seem to have much affection for the idle rich. I take it you grew up in the huddled masses that put in an honest day for their honest pay."

"Something like that."

Dianna's voice carried a sharp edge as she spoke. "My father never worked a day in his life."

Dylan noticed the hard light that had entered her eyes. He felt that discussing her father would only lead them into an abyss of bitterness. "Mine worked like a mule."

"What did he do, pull a plow?" The hard light faded from her eyes.

"Worse than that; he worked on the waterfront, longshoreman . . . mostly over at the Robin Street Wharf." Dylan wondered where this "chance" meeting was taking him and whether he could handle the mental gymnastics necessary for a relationship with this complex young woman. And he was now convinced beyond any reasonable doubt that she would provide the key to whoever and whatever was behind the execution-style murders of South Louisiana's mayors.

"A longshoreman . . ." Dianna gave him a thoughtful look. "I have an idea he was much more than that."

"He was to me . . . and my mother," Dylan agreed, "but to most people, he was just another dumb dock worker." He heard again the schoolyard taunts from the recesses of his memory.

Dianna glanced at Dylan's wedding ring, a plain gold band gleaming dully in the fading light. "How long have you been married, Dylan St. John?"

Dylan, for reasons he couldn't explain, felt that Dianna already knew more about him than he wanted her to know, and he was unwilling to tell her more. "Does it matter?"

"I guess not." She shrugged and gazed across the lagoon at the lights winking on in the museum's colonnade. "It's nice here with the breeze off the water . . . nature's air conditioning. And the sounds of the city seem so far away."

Glancing at the soft dark hair swirling about her face in a sudden gust of wind, Dylan realized that he would have to create a distance between himself and this enigmatic and striking woman far greater than the three feet of stone separating them on the park bench.

8

"Tin Roof Blues"

"So there you are!" The disembodied voice sounded like iron scraping granite.

Dylan glanced over his shoulder at the white-haired giant stalking toward them from the deep shadows of the live oaks.

"Hello, Matthias," Dianna said casually. "I thought you would have gone home by now." Her voice was flat, emotionless.

The giant, gripping his heavy ax by its haft resting over his shoulder, stood in front of Dylan. Glancing at Dianna, he said, "Who's *this?*"

Dianna gave him a hard smile that softened when she turned toward Dylan. "Dylan — meet Matthias Teague. Matthias, this is Dylan St. John."

Dylan stood up to shake hands. The top of his head barely cleared Teague's shoulders. "Nice," he said, thinking what a foolish word to use in a confrontational situation like this one, "to meet you."

"Same here," Teague said and extended his meaty hand.

Seeing Teague's thick lips curling into a half-smile, Dylan knew what Teague planned to do: the same thing most men do, who trust supremely in their physical prowess, when introduced to possible rivals. Dylan thrust his own hand quickly into the thick webbing between Teague's thumb and forefinger, making it impossible for him to exert the crushing pressure he so obviously wanted to.

Dianna had surely seen Teague's reaction in similar circumstances. "I'm sure you boys will become fast friends — in time, of course."

Sitting back down on the bench, Dylan held Teague's stare, noticing the metallic-like glint in his eyes.

"Matthias was a navy seal, Dylan," Dianna said conversationally, smiling at the big man. "He learned dozens of ways to kill other human beings."

"That's absolutely correct," Teague agreed and grinned down at Dylan. "You spend any time in the service?"

Dylan nodded, feeling trapped by the big man who now stood close to the bench as though cutting off any possible chance he might have for escape. The lights from the museum glanced off the blade of the ax. *This is stupid! Why would somebody I just met take a swipe at me with an ax? Don't let your imagination get the best of you, St. John.*

"Oh yeah," Teague continued, seemingly at home with the new subject of conversation. "What branch?"

Seeing there was no way to avoid answering, Dylan said, "Marines."

It didn't take long to begin. "Marines!" Teague repeated the word as though he had mispronounced it the first time. "Marines! You guys are the most overrated bunch in the history of war!" He unslung his ax. With a snap of his wrist, he buried it in a tree twenty feet away. "Every jarhead thinks he's another John Wayne storming the beach at Iwo Jima."

Dylan saw absolutely no point in allowing Teague to intimidate him into a heated argument that was doomed to stalemate from the very outset.

Teague appeared to take Dylan's silence as a taunt. "You make it over to Nam?"

"Can't you see he's not interested in participating in your military fantasies, Matthias?" Dianna interrupted.

"Fantasies!" Teague was incensed by the word. "You think fighting with the Riverine Forces down in the Delta was some kind of fantasy, you rich little snot?" But he mistakenly kept his eyes on Dylan as he spoke.

Dianna uncoiled from the bench, kicking Teague solidly in the left kneecap, all in one smooth motion before he could defend himself. He leaned over from the waist, his hands clutching the damaged knee and bellowed in pain. A split second later, Dianna, using her locked hands and a vicious shoulder rotation, whacked him on the left ear. Off balance on one foot, his hands still cradling the damaged knee, Teague crashed to the ground.

Standing above him, hands on her rounded hips, Dianna spoke between clenched teeth in a voice edged with ground glass. "You get up right now and go home, Matthias Teague. We'll talk about this tomorrow!"

Teague's confident and fiery spirit had been thoroughly doused. He pushed himself stiffly to his feet, averting his eyes from Dianna and Dylan. Then he limped painfully over to his ax embedded deeply in the tree, worked it free, and disappeared into the shadowed grove of trees.

Breathing heavily, Dianna stood with her hands still propped on her hips, staring out into the quiet park. After what was apparently her cooling-down period, she walked back to the bench and sat down beside Dylan, leaving only twelve inches of stone bench between them this time.

For some reason he could not explain, Dylan was more astonished at Dianna's quickness than he was at the viciousness of her attack on Teague. He had never seen a woman, and very few men, who could move that fast. Part of it, he knew, was assuredly born of hours and days and years of sweat and training in health clubs and martial-arts studios. But no matter how much work goes into it, a person must be born with the potential for that kind of feline like speed and agility.

Taking a deep breath, Dianna let it out slowly and stared off across the lagoon. "I apologize for that little scene, Dylan. Matthias can sometimes be quite rude."

Dylan could feel the tension in the air as thick as a bayou mist. "Remind me never to call you a rich little snot."

Dianna gave him a sharp glance, then her face softened. She threw her head back and laughed, and the sound of it was as true and honest as a hard day's work.

Something happened then. Dylan could tell a barrier had been crossed, although he didn't know what the barrier was made of or what lay on the other side. He did know that he had moved closer to the trade winds of Dianna's life; a little closer to the reasons for her violent temper, her little-girl affections; and most of all, the reasons why three men had died senseless and violent deaths.

As Dylan watched her, the laughter faded and disappeared like the flattened orange ball sinking beyond the great, muddy sweep of the river. "You think ol' Matthias might need to go to the emergency room?"

"Ol' Matthias *is* an emergency," Dianna said, her smile bright in the tangle of dark hair. "All he needs is a little *room*." The nonsensical words set her off laughing again.

Dylan laughed with her, although he had a nagging sense that her reactions bordered on the maniacal.

Dianna's laughter finally played itself out again. She wiped her eyes with both forefingers, then brushed her hair back with her fingertips. "I think I could grow to like you, Dylan St. John," she said, glancing down at his left hand, "in spite of that little gold band wrapping itself around your finger."

This was part of the uncharted territory Dylan expected to enter, and he hoped that his compass was in working order. "You're kind of nice to be around yourself. Almost like the kid sister I never had."

She flinched slightly at the "kid sister"

comparison, then lifted her feet up on the bench, turning toward him, hugging her knees. "What kind of work do you do?"

"I'm a representative for a business up north," he said quickly. Although the "business" was law enforcement and "north" was only seventy miles upriver, the half-truths somehow made the deception easier for Dylan to live with.

"Sounds mysterious."

"Nah. It's actually pretty boring stuff most of the time — same old routine day after day."

"And the other times ?"

"The other times are paydays."

Dianna smiled again. "Maybe we could go to a movie one night."

"Maybe."

"How long are you going to be in town?"

Dylan tried to fight against the feeling that he was actually betraying Susan. As he spoke he kept her image in mind, nicely framed on the writing desk next to his typewriter. "Depends. I never know if it'll take a few days or a few weeks to finish my business."

"Why don't we go see *Little Big Man*? It's playing over at the Saenger."

"Dustin Hoffman." Dylan felt like a kid fumbling around for the right words. "I saw the ad in the *Picayune*."

"Or maybe you'd like *Five Easy Pieces* better. I think it's at the Orpheum."

Dianna spun smoothly on the bench, placing her feet on the ground. Leaning over, she picked up a Popsicle stick and began writing in the dust. Dylan could barely make out the street address and apartment number. She gave him time to memorize it, then next to it she wrote a telephone number.

Resuming her position on the bench, she said, "Think you can remember them?"

Dylan nodded.

They sat on their bench and talked about the ordinary things men and women who have just met talk about. Around them the twilight drifted through the trees like a purple mist. After a long while they walked together through the oak grove back to the deserted festival grounds.

"I should have known he wouldn't go home," Dianna said. She stared at a red Ford pickup parked at the curb beneath a streetlight, then said with a sigh, "I'd give you a lift, but Matthias might not be the best of company under the circumstances."

Dylan took the hand she offered him, feeling its softness and warmth and her reluctance to leave as she held his gaze with an expression that bordered on serenity. "It's such a nice night, I think I'll walk awhile," he answered.

"Good-night then."

The sound of her words lingered as he watched her walk toward the truck. Then he found his way back to the blue Volkswagen parked on a side street, cranked the engine, turned on the radio, and listened to Simon and Garfunkel sing the last verse of "Bridge Over Troubled Water."

Dylan took a pencil and note pad from the glove compartment and wrote down Dianna's address and phone number. As the steady engine idled, his thoughts fastened on Dianna Salazar and Matthias Teague. He wondered how far Teague would go to exorcise the demons that tormented him. Slipping the gearshift into first, he pulled away from the curb and set his course toward Evangeline.

"This is the break we've been looking for!" Emile paced slowly back and forth in his office, making an occasional gesture with his coffee mug. Several spots on his tan uniform testified to the fact that the mug was only half empty.

After a few hours' sleep in his own bed, Dylan had asked Susan to come to the office with him that afternoon. "I can't guarantee yet that these are the people involved, but they're sure way out front of everybody else," Dylan said.

Susan, wearing her first maternity dress, a short-sleeved cotton shift the color of the yellow June sunshine spilling through the window, said matter-of-factly, "You'll have to go then." Her eyes remained fixed on a tiny English sparrow perched in a crepe myrtle outside the window.

Emile walked over to the desk, sat down in his squeaky chair, and asked, "You two have already talked about this?"

Dylan nodded. Taking off his navy sport coat, he tossed it on the coatrack next to the door. "I thought the possibility of my staying down there was pretty good."

"Whenever one of my men goes on an assignment like this where he'll be away from home for a while," Emile said as Susan turned from the window, "I always like to bring his wife in on it."

Emile glanced at Dylan, then continued. "A man's not going to be much good if his wife's against his taking a job that keeps him out of town." He spoke in a calm, reassuring voice, explaining to Susan, "He'd have his mind on his wife and family and not on his work. That's a liability in any business — but it's especially true in this one."

Dylan knew that *liability* was the closest Emile was going to get to using the word *dangerous*. He watched Susan's reaction. Her face remained calm. She even gave him a smile while Emile was speaking to her.

When Emile was finished, he asked Susan, "Well, what do you think?"

"I think the same thing I did before you started talking," she said as she turned to Dylan. "You'll have to go."

"There's really not much to it," Dylan said, not believing his own words. "Since I've already gotten acquainted with them, it'll just be a matter of keeping an eye on them to see if I can come up with anything that might be useful."

A sharp rapping sounded on the door. "Come on in," Emile called.

Elaine's freckled face, aglow with the prospect of spending money, appeared around the door frame. "You about ready to leave, Susan?"

"You think the stores in Bon Marche Mall can handle the three of us?" Susan asked as she stood up to leave, slipping her purse over her shoulder.

"We're certainly going to find out," Elaine answered and smiled. "C'mon, Emma's probably got three or four ballpoints already warmed up to write checks on Emile's account."

Susan walked into Dylan's arms, placed the fingertips of her left hand on his cheek, and kissed him warmly on the mouth. "Be careful," she whispered.

Dylan stared into her clear green eyes, which revealed only a shadow of concern. "I'll be home as soon as I can — probably three or four days. And I'll call you every night."

With a quick smile, she joined Elaine. "Let's go then. I can't *wait* to see all those pretty lacy dresses and bonnets and those precious little sleepers."

"You don't want to buy too much just yet," Elaine cautioned, as they went out the door. "We're giving you a baby shower in a few months."

When the door closed with a click, Emile got up and walked over to the coffee service, poured himself a cup, and stared out the window. The light cast the near side of his face into shadow. "We can't let the governor's task force know about this, Dylan."

"I know."

Emile continued as though he had to convince himself that his decision was the best thing to do. "That woman's got too much political clout."

"New Orleans is infamous for protecting its own — the ones fortunate enough to be inside the power structure anyway," Dylan added, "and it doesn't matter much what they've done. I know," he added. "I grew up there."

"The police department wouldn't protect a known murderer," Emile reassured himself out loud. "A cop's a cop, and it doesn't matter whether he's got *New Orleans* or *New York* on his badge." He turned, his intense gaze on Dylan. "The problem we're gonna run into is this," he said, taking a swallow of coffee, then setting his cup on a table nearby. "Nobody down there would ever believe that the mayor's daughter or any of her friends could possibly be involved in something like these murders."

He walked over to his desk and sat down. "So the investigation would never get off the ground." Glancing at the cup he had left sitting on the table, Emile finished his brief summation. "Either that or her father would keep the police from ever finding out that the possibility even existed."

Dylan picked up Emile's coffee cup and carried it over to his desk. "I'll have to find a way to keep close to them." He handed the cup to Emile. "Dianna's as wild and unpredictable as anybody you've ever seen, but she does seem to have a normal side to her."

Sitting down on the edge of the desk, Dylan expressed his thoughts out loud as much for himself as to let Emile know what the situation was. "This guy Teague, though —" He saw again the image of those pale, emotionless eyes. "He really gives me the creeps."

"Big and mean, huh?"

Dylan glanced down at Emile, remembering he had discussed Teague briefly with him on the phone when he had gotten in from New Orleans. "I'd say that's probably an understatement for this guy."

"I've got just the thing for you in case Mr. Teague feels compelled to act out the darker side of his obviously stunted personality." Emile grinned at Dylan and said, "Learned that in a workshop the old sheriff sent me to years ago. Are you duly impressed?"

"I think I'd be more impressed if you had something I could handle Teague with."

Emile reached down and opened his bottom desk drawer. Lifting out his *Teague-handler*, he placed it on an empty manila folder in front of him and unfolded the cloth. Dark with Three-in-One Oil, the heavy cotton cloth had kept the blue steel of the automatic in mint condition. "Ain't it a beauty?" He picked the pistol up and let it lay flat in the palm of his hand. "Army issue Colt .45. I carried it in North Africa in '43."

Dylan took the weapon by the grip, feeling the solid, reassuring heft of it. "Looks like it just came from the factory."

"There's a nick or two on it, but it's as dependable as they come." He shoved two clips still in their cloth wrapping across the desk toward Dylan, then took a full box of ammunition from the drawer and placed it next to them. "You ever shoot one of these?"

"A little in boot camp," Dylan answered, locking back the receiver. "A lot more overseas."

"Good. It takes some getting used to, but then you already know what a wallop it packs."

Dylan turned the pistol toward daylight and looked down the barrel. "Clean as a whistle. Not a speck of rust."

Emile swallowed the last of his coffee thoughtfully while Dylan opened the box of ammunition and filled both clips. He slapped one home, checked the safety, and put the pistol and extra clip away in their cloth wrapping.

"Guess I'm ready."

"Where you planning to stay?"

"At my mother's, I guess. The department

won't have to pay for a hotel room, and besides, the food's good."

"I've got a better idea," Emile said as he fished a house key out of his shirt pocket and tossed it over to Dylan.

"What's this for?"

"Friend of mine, Sam Romano, owns the St. Louis Grocery on the corner of Dauphine and St. Louis Streets."

"I know it," Dylan said, intrigued by Emile's network of friends. "It's a block off Bourbon."

"Right. Anyhow, he owes me a favor or two, so I called him last night, and he said you could use the apartment above the grocery store." Emile stood up and stretched.

"You sure he won't mind? He doesn't even know me."

"He knows *me*," Emile said, as if that should settle everything — and for Dylan it did. "Besides, he lives out on the lakefront now. He and his wife almost never use the apartment anymore."

After a thoughtful minute, Emile said, "One more thing, Dylan."

"What's that?"

"You're going there for surveillance. Get enough evidence to break this thing, and then we'll send the right people in with the firepower. Don't try to be a hero."

"I'm not the hero type, Emile."

"Just be careful."

Dylan thought of Susan, his mother, and now Emile sending him off with the same words. "I'm on my way then," he said, feeling a reluctance to trade the peace and casual ease of Evangeline for the mean streets of New Orleans, where he imagined Matthias Teague waiting for him like some hulking wild animal.

Dylan parked his Volkswagen on St. Louis Street halfway down the block toward Burgundy and walked back to the grocery store. The front door opened at an angle beneath the balcony and faced the intersection of Dauphine and St. Louis. Slanting sunlight threw the shadows of the buildings halfway across the street. Dylan stopped on the sidewalk, peered through the doorway for a few seconds, then walked into the store's shadowy interior.

The smell of hoop cheese and plums and grapes greeted him as he entered. Several rows of shelves were laden with canned goods and snacks and toilet articles. A short man with dark hair parted in the middle, wearing brown slacks and a crisp white shirt, walked the narrow aisles filling a plastic shopping basket.

To the right of the entrance stood a counter holding candy and gum and a big green cash register. On the wall behind it, shelves overflowed with cigarettes. Mardi Gras posters and cardboard advertisements were hung and plastered everywhere, making the store's interior an incomprehensible jumble of brightly colored pictures and words. From a tinny-sounding black plastic radio on a shelf behind the cluttered counter, a Dixieland band played "Tin Roof Blues."

"You must be St. John," the man behind the counter stated flatly.

His eyes having grown accustomed to the gloom, Dylan noticed a burly man with curly gray hair sitting on a stool behind the cash register. A short, thin, slightly curved nose sat not quite centered in his dark face. His brown eyes, crinkling at the corners, made Dylan think of Santa Claus in the old Coca Cola advertisements. "Yes sir. Mr. Romano?"

The man nodded. "Emile said you'd be coming in today. Excuse me a minute — grab yourself a Coke or something." Turning his head, Romano spoke to his only customer. "Morning, Ed. How you feeling? Find everything you need?"

Dylan opened the lid of the floor cooler just inside the door, took a bottle of Coke out of the near-freezing water it stood in, and popped the top off in the built-in opener on the side of the box. As he drank, he watched Romano bag the groceries and ring up the sale, never leaving his stool.

"See you tomorrow, Ed," Romano said. He waved as his reticent customer left the store.

Dylan watched the customer shuffle across the intersection, then observed, "Ed's not much of a talker, is he?"

"One of his *good* points," Romano said. He kept to his stool while he talked. "So you're going to be staying with us awhile."

"If that's all right."

"Emile and I go way back," Romano stated, as if that was answer enough. He took a cigar the size of a small sapling out of a box beneath the counter, peeled off the cellophane, and stuck it into the corner of his mouth. "He told me a little bit about why you're down here."

"And you *still* don't mind?" Dylan thought Emile must be a very good friend, or Romano owed him a favor that he had no other way of repaying.

Romano chewed thoughtfully on his thick cigar. "The Salazar girl lives here in the Quarter, but then you already know that."

Dylan remembered that the address she

had scratched in the dirt was only three or four blocks from the store. He asked, "You know much about her?"

"Only what I read in the papers over the years," Romano answered, squinting in the glare from the open door. "That, and the gossip that's always traveling in New Orleans political circles. She moved down here to the Quarter a couple of years ago."

"You *know* her?" Dylan felt he was about to pick up another piece of the intricate and confusing puzzle that formed the portrait of Dianna Salazar.

Romano chomped his cigar with renewed vigor. "She comes in once in a while." He took a white handkerchief from his back pocket and mopped his forehead. "Muskrat Ramble" poured from the plastic radio. "That girl's crazy. Or maybe she just gets a big kick out of acting like she is. Either way, if you ask me, her cornbread ain't quite cooked."

Stuffing his handkerchief back in his pocket, Romano went back to his discourse on Dianna. "You wanna know what she did? I'll tell you what she did," he continued without waiting for an answer. "Couple of months ago, she was standing right there," he said as he pointed to the spot where Ed had stood a minute or two earlier. "A cockroach — and I mean a big, ugly one — crawled out from under the register."

Romano took the ragged cigar from between his teeth and pointed it at Dylan. "I was about to take my shoe off to kill it and you know what that pretty little woman did?" Again he didn't wait for the answer to his question. "She reached out with her cute little thumb before I could move, and she mashed that thing to mush!"

A sound of disgust erupted from deep down in Romano's throat. "I mean with her thumb! I ain't never seen that before, and I been killing roaches all my life. My wife has a fit when she just *sees* one running across the kitchen linoleum."

Dylan had to admit that it took an unusual woman to do a thing like that. "Anything else?"

"Yeah. She grinned at me like she was hearing somebody tell a funny joke the whole time she was doing it," Romano said before tossing his soggy cigar into a green garbage can at the end of the counter. "I'll feel better when she moves away from here. A lot of her neighbors feel the same way."

9

The Seven Seas

The tall man walked out into the street, his hand loosely dangling above the .44 resting in its low-slung holster. Twenty yards away, another man stopped, facing him. The grim, craggy face of the tall man gave no indication of the thoughts behind his narrowed eyes. Suddenly his hand whipped down and forward as two shots rang out almost simultaneously.

Dylan got up from the lumpy sofa and flicked the knob on the television. The black-and-white picture faded to a pinpoint of white light. He carried his metal tray into the kitchen area, pulling the curtain beneath the sink aside, and dumped the brown paper wrappings of his oyster po'boy into the garbage.

Switching off the fluorescent light over the sink, he walked into the tiny bedroom off the kitchen and tried out the sagging mattress on the double bed. It was even more uncomfortable than it looked. *Ah well, at least I don't have to pay for a bad night's sleep.* He got up and took only a few minutes to unpack his duffel bag and put his things away in the antique bureau, coffin-sized closet, and the bathroom's mirrored medicine cabinet.

Returning to the living room, Dylan opened the French doors and stepped out onto the balcony. Floored with narrow cypress boards and constructed with a galvanized roof and scrolled-iron railing and posts, it wrapped around the corner of the building. He walked along the Dauphine Street side to the end, where the balcony swung around to the front on St. Louis Street. Testing the chains first, he sat down in a porch swing.

Gazing down Dauphine toward Canal four blocks away, he saw the glare of the storefronts and the lighted windows of office buildings rising against the night sky. Below him the tourists, along with the Quarter's permanent residents, had begun their nightly revelry. Laughter, squeals of delight, and bits of coarse conversation drifted up to him from street level. Far off a tugboat whistle moaned like a wayward soul lost in the thick fog banks above the sweeping flow of the great river.

Only a few hours gone, and I already miss her. Dylan wondered if his job was worth being away from Susan and his soon-to-be-born first child. He stood up and leaned on the railing where it curved around the corner of the building. Below him the drinkers and sightseers ambled along the sidewalks and out into the streets. A block closer to the river, down St. Louis Street, the blaring jazz, thumping rhythm-and-blues, bellowing bedlam, and smoky glare of Bourbon Street had set in for the night.

Dylan thought of the little cabin on the edge of the Atchafalaya Basin and of Susan sitting next to him on their dock at the end of the moon's shining path across the water. Then he went inside the apartment, picked up the heavy black phone, and dialed. The phone rang only once before the person on the other end answered.

"Hello."

"Hi. Thought you might want to take in that movie."

"Is that you, Dylan?" Dianna's voice had a breathless quality, as though she had been running. "I didn't know if I'd ever hear from you again."

"Why are you so out of breath?"

"Working out," she said, taking a deep breath. "Gotta keep my figure, you know."

Dylan fought a strong and sudden urge to slam the receiver down. He felt anger welling up inside him and could not pin down the reason for it. "Well, what do you say?"

"Oh, the movie. Sure."

Dylan listened to the sound of her swallowing something to drink at the other end of the telephone line.

"Why don't you come around in thirty minutes or so. We're not dressing, are we?"

"I'm not."

"In New Orleans, you never know."

"See you soon."

Hanging up the receiver more gently than he needed to, Dylan took a deep breath and exhaled slowly. He glanced down at his white shirt and khakis that Susan had so carefully ironed that morning. Then he walked into the kitchen, ran the tap water to fill a red plastic cup, and drank it down. He combed his hair back with his fingers and rubbed the stubble on his chin with the side of his forefinger as he headed toward the bathroom to shave.

"How'd you like the movie?" Dianna, wearing penny loafers, a green plaid skirt, and a white cotton blouse with a Peter Pan collar, looked as though she had stepped out of an advertisement for a parochial girl's school.

Dylan gazed at the vendors, tourists,

drunks, street hustlers, elegantly dressed couples, bell-bottomed hippies, and other late-night visitors to the Jackson Square Area as they walked along Decatur Street. "Nicholson never was one of my favorites. I liked the character he played even less."

Dianna let her hand trail along the tall piked iron fence that surrounded the parklike area of the square. "I thought he was kind of attractive in a strange sort of way."

"An elitist snob from a rich family going slumming with the Texas rednecks," Dylan said with disgust, suddenly realizing that he could have been talking about one of Dianna's little company of friends.

"I think the movie wanted to show how people can be wounded by society even if they do come from wealthy backgrounds," Dianna said thoughtfully. Her voice had taken on a childlike softness that Dylan hadn't heard before.

"Looked to me like his wounds were self-inflicted," Dylan continued, feeling that he might break down Dianna's defenses; draw her out into the open. "And it was pretty obvious he didn't care one way or the other whether he *wounded* other people. He was like a lot of people who grow up coddled and pampered; they're just children grown old."

Dianna stopped abruptly, glaring at Dylan. "What do you know about what money does to people, you blue collar tr. . . !" She let her words trail off. She turned away and stared through the heavy bars of the fence at the lighted spires of St. Louis Cathedral on the other side of the square.

"Trash," Dylan said softly. "Is *that* the word you're looking for? Go ahead and say it." He despised the game he was playing, then remembered Jimmy Iverson lying beneath six feet of Feliciana clay. "Go ahead and *say* it. I've been called worse."

Dianna spun around with that catlike quickness Dylan had seen at the lagoon. Taking his hands, she said in a voice touched with remorse, "I'm *so* sorry, Dylan!" Her eyes were bright and moist. "I didn't mean that."

She's either a great actress or I hit a soft spot. "Forget it. Let's get some coffee," he said and motioned toward the Cafe du Monde across the street.

"Okay." Dianna brushed at her eyes with the backs of her fingers. "But let's go someplace else first."

"Suits me. What do you have in mind?"

"The Seven Seas."

"Never heard of it." Dylan noticed that the hard light in her eyes had died away.

"But then, it's been a long time since I lived down here."

"It's . . . different," Dianna offered by way of description, "and it's only a few blocks away." She smiled up at him, slipping her hand inside his arm as they strolled along the narrow streets of the Quarter like any young couple on a first date.

The Rolling Stones were singing the praises of a "Honky Tonk Woman" when Dylan ushered Dianna through the door of The Seven Seas. He wondered if the blue-white haze of smoke inside left any room for oxygen. "This is *different*, all right," he said, but saw that Dianna hadn't heard a word above the blaring jukebox.

Next to the span of plate glass in a front alcove that could have once been used as a display window, two young men sat across from each other staring at the chess pieces on the board between them. A study in the art of motionlessness, they gave the impression of mannequins abandoned by a previous tenant.

A long bar on the left, cluttered with glasses, bottles, packs of cigarettes, matchbooks, ashtrays, and loose change duplicated itself in the long mirror that ran the length of wall. The assortment of people seated on cushioned metal stools could have been labeled "Theater of the Strange." They ran the gamut of human shapes and wore an interesting array of boots and sandals; tattered bell-bottoms and long, wrinkled skirts; beads and bracelets and bangles of every conceivable shape and size. Their bodies bore tattoos of amazing creativity and scars of dubious origin. A few still possessed all their teeth.

Dianna shoved her way next to the bar, waving at the bartender. "Hey, 'Chrome Dome'! Give me a glass of white wine and . . ." She spoke over her shoulder, "What are you drinking?"

"Sasparilla."

"What?"

"Bad joke. A Coke."

". . . and a Coke."

Five minutes later the harried bartender brought their drinks. Dylan needed no explanation as to his nickname. A bright silver circle had been painted on top of the man's completely hairless head. A bushy black beard streaked with more silver paint and silver eyeshadow completed the creative cosmetic wonder labeled "Chrome Dome."

Dylan dropped a five on the bar. The bartender grabbed it, stuffed it into an inside pocket of his white apron, and walked off toward the thirsty patrons at the far end of the bar who were howling for more drinks.

As it was obvious no change would be forthcoming, Dylan picked up his Coke and turned to leave.

"Wait a minute!" Dianna's quick anger was returning for an encore. "He can't get away with that!"

Dylan glanced at the silver-topped man dispensing drinks to what appeared to be several characters out of a Kafka short story. "Yes he can."

Dianna relented, interestingly enough without protest. "All right. We'll never get a place to sit down in here. Let's go out to the patio."

As Dylan followed Dianna toward the rear of the bar, the jukebox changed its tune. *I'm giving you a love that's true, so get ready, get ready.*

Enclosed by the walls of adjoining buildings, the rear patio was small and crowded but seemed to attract a different type — quieter, given to wine rather than hard liquor, and obviously more acquainted with soap and water.

Two women in their early twenties wearing tailored suits, minus the jackets that hung over a low sweet olive limb, played Ping-Pong on a table standing in the patio's center. They had also slipped out of their shoes and bounced about on the bricks in stocking feet, slapping the white ball back and forth with sandpaper-sided paddles.

Dylan and Dianna sat together on a low stucco wall and watched the ebb and flow of the game.

"You like it better back here?" Dianna asked, engrossed in the competition.

Unable to get the image of "Chrome Dome" out of his mind, Dylan missed her question. "Why does he paint himself silver like that?"

"Who?"

Dylan's head turned toward Dianna. "Who? You mean you know more than one person with a silver head?"

"Just kidding!" Dianna's clear, honest laughter spilled out of her as though she had been storing it up for a very long time. "I don't *know* why. Why are we fighting in Vietnam? Why do politicians *talk* about everything and never *say* anything? *Why* isn't Ted Kennedy in jail? *Why* —"

"I get the point," Dylan said, shutting off the tirade.

"Hey, they're finished." Dianna pulled her black pumps off and set them on the wall. "Wanna try a game?" she said, walking over to the table.

"Why would I want to play Ping-Pong? *Why* —"

"That's enough, you." Dianna grinned, grabbed a paddle, and tossed it to him.

Dylan slipped his navy sport coat off and laid it next to Dianna's shoes. Then he walked around to the other side of the table. "Go ahead, you serve." Knees flexed, paddle held toward the backhand side, he got ready to return.

"Ten bucks says I take you." Without waiting for a reply, she made a scissors motion with her hands, the ball clicking on the surface of the plywood table.

Making a quick stab with the paddle, Dylan watched the ball clear the net by half an inch and dribble off the right side of the table like melting ice. "Where'd you learn a serve like that? I don't think it's legal."

While he critiqued her shot, Dianna slammed another serve down the opposite side of the table, the ball catching the very edge. Dylan made a reflex backhand, but saw the ball carom off his paddle, landing twenty feet away on the brick patio. Ten minutes later the score was 21–9, and Dianna tossed her paddle into the air with a shout of victory.

Dylan flipped his paddle onto the table and walked over for his jacket. He tried to kid himself that the loss hadn't stung his pride, but it wasn't working. "Nice game," he said, watching Dianna slip her shoes on.

"I won a trophy once, too," she boasted. She gave him a sly smile, then stood up, her face slightly flushed. "When I was a junior in high school. Table tennis, city champ."

Still smarting from the loss, Dylan found himself saying, "Next time we play *real* tennis." *What am I doing? I'm supposed to be working on a multiple-homicide case, and here I am, worrying about getting beat in a stupid game of Ping-Pong!*

"I think not," Dianna replied quickly, taking a sip of her wine. "I saw you play at LSU, remember?"

Dylan put his jacket back on and picked up his Coke from the low stucco wall. Taking a big swallow, he glanced at Dianna. "Well, what's next?"

"Wanna arm wrestle?" She held her hand out as though to challenge him, then dropped her arm, smiled, and sipped her wine.

"I don't think I could take another whipping this soon," Dylan said, more than a little troubled to find that he was enjoying the evening. "Maybe we should go on home."

"Coffee and beignets first?" Her words were a plea. "I think it's the law for a first date in New Orleans." She finished her wine, placed the glass on top of the wall, and took his arm. "After all, we certainly don't want to break any laws . . . do we?"

Dylan felt a stab of guilt when Dianna spoke the word *date*, but he made no effort to stop her as she held his arm as they made their way to the street.

The two Pontalba Apartment buildings located on St. Ann and St. Peter Streets flanking opposite sides of Jackson Square were said to be the oldest in the country. Iron columns and delicate wrought-iron balustrades adorned these residential row buildings constructed of brick in 1848–1850.

Dianna's balcony on St. Ann commanded a view of the river, the square, St. Louis Cathedral, and the Cabildo. Fifty years older than the Pontalba, the Cabildo served as the seat of Louisiana territorial government for France, Spain, the Confederacy, and the United States.

Dianna, sipping her café au lait, sat across from Dylan at a glass-topped iron table on her balcony. A white saucer between them contained smears of powdered sugar and brown bits of crust, the remains of an order of beignets. "Now this is nicer than being down there with all those noisy people, isn't it?"

Dylan glanced down and to his left at the glare of the Cafe du Monde, its army of black-coated waiters bustling among the tables with laden trays. "I think it's probably a little less noisy than The Seven Seas," he said, remembering the din of shouted conversations and the thunderous jukebox they had just left behind.

"Exactly," Dianna agreed, gazing up at the starry night. "After twenty or thirty minutes in that place, you've reached your noise quota for the whole month. Even the murmuring drone down at Cafe du Monde is too much."

Dianna folded her hands in an attitude of prayer, resting her smooth chin on the tips of her forefingers. "I'm so glad we met, Dylan."

"I am, too." Dylan willed himself not to look at his wedding band. "You're a nice girl, Dianna."

"Nice girl?" She blinked, then blinked once more. "How did you get down to New Orleans — on a time machine from Victorian England?"

Dylan noticed the almost pained look in her eyes. "That's a compliment, in case you're wondering," he offered. "Maybe we can get together again."

"When?" Dianna seemed confused, taken

off guard by the *nice girl* comment.

"How about tomorrow night?"

Her face brightened. "That would be —" she stopped, her eyes narrowed, turning toward the thick darkness gathered in the live oaks beyond the square's piked fence. "No — no, I can't. Not tomorrow night. I've got to . . . go out of town."

Then she brushed her thoughts aside. "But the night after would be just fine."

Dylan had seen the shadows flickering in Dianna's eyes as she spoke. It occurred to him that he would be making that same out-of-town trip. "Good. Maybe you can show me a good place to eat. I'm sure things have changed since I moved."

"How long have you been gone?"

Dylan thought back to that dreary September day when he and his mother had stopped at his father's grave on the way to the bus station. "About ten years now."

"You never *did* tell me where you live," Dianna said as an after-thought.

"Across the river from Baton Rouge."

She gave him a suspicious glance and said, "Well, that really narrows it down! Houston, Phoenix, Seattle . . . they're *all* across the river from Baton Rouge."

Dylan smiled at the way her bottom lip pushed forward like a scolded child. "In a little cabin out close to the Basin."

"Sounds romantic."

This was the treacherous water Dylan knew to avoid. "Probably bore you to death in about two days."

"Maybe not." The light in Dianna's eyes softened. "It might prove just the opposite."

Dylan pushed his chair back. "Well, I guess I better get going. Work tomorrow and all that." He led the way through the curtained French doors leading into her living room.

At her door, she let her hands trail at her sides, leaning her shoulders back against the wall as she gazed up at him. "Until day after tomorrow then."

Dylan looked briefly into the smoky depths of her eyes, then opened the door and left, calling back over his shoulder, "See you then."

Downstairs, he walked along St. Ann enjoying the mild June night. He glanced toward the Cabildo. In its shadowed archway, a tall figure stood staring at him. He recognized the white cropped hair and the almost luminous eyes. The light of the street lamp flashed on the blade of a big knife as he stroked it back and forth on a whetstone in his hand.

"Nothing very interesting. Just finding out as much as I can about these people." Dylan stood in the open French doors, holding the phone in one hand, gazing out at the midnight city as he assured his wife that he was all right.

At the other end of the phone line, Susan adjusted her pillow against the headboard and lay back against it. The lamp on her nightstand cast its amber glow across her Bible's pages with passages underlined and margin notes written in her neat script. "Are you sure there's nothing dangerous about this?"

"Nothing to it," Dylan said, seeing the image of Teague's gleaming knife blade in the shadowed archway. "I'm just trying to come up with some hard evidence so we can get the *real* law enforcement people in here."

"If you aren't real enough for them, why don't you just come on home?"

Dylan smiled at Susan's ability to cut straight through all his attempts at clouding issues. He couldn't tell her that some of the *real* cops might end up on the wrong side of the law. "I don't have enough experience to take this investigation all the way through on my own. I just happened by a stroke of good fortune to meet some people who might help us get a break."

He remembered recognizing one or two New Orleans cops from the governor's task force at the Camelot Festival. He knew they had to be looking for suspects in the killings, but would have recognized the mayor's daughter and immediately ruled her out as a suspect.

"When are you coming home?"

"In a couple of days, I hope. I'll call you tomorrow."

PART THREE

Starlight

10

The Visit

Susan lifted the mobile from the white box, unfolded it from its tissue paper wrappings, and held it aloft. The colorful ceramic figures of Winnie-the-Pooh, Christopher Robin, and other characters who lived in the Hundred Acre Wood turned slowly, catching the morning light streaming in through the window. *What baby could resist falling in love with these little fellows?*

After a few minutes of examining the figures in detail, Susan replaced them in the box and set it on the coffee table. She fluffed up the pillows on the flowered sofa, finished her dusting in the living room, and mopped the kitchen floor. Then, putting the copper kettle to boil on the gas stove, she sat down at the little Formica dinette in the kitchen.

Opening her Bible, Susan read: *For we are to God the aroma of Christ among those who are being saved and those who are perishing. To the one we are the smell of death; to the other, the fragrance of life.*

At that moment Susan heard the rumble of a big engine and the sound of tires crunching in the shells on the shoulder of the blacktop road. Walking to the window, she pushed aside the checked yellow-and-white curtains. She saw a red Ford pickup parked on the shoulder of the road on the close side of the tin-roofed building that served as garage, boathouse, and storage shed.

The glare on the windshield made it impossible to recognize the driver, but as the door opened and he got out, Susan knew that she had never seen this tall, broad-shouldered man before. His whitish-blonde hair was cropped short and his skin had reddened rather than tanned in the blazing South Louisiana sunshine. He wore heavy black boots that looked as wide as crossties, black jeans, and a sleeveless orange T-shirt that revealed the heavy corded muscles of his arms.

Susan felt a chill at the back of her neck, shook it off, and said out loud, "This is silly! Why should I be afraid of someone I don't even know? This is Evangeline. He's probably just somebody asking directions."

Keeping her eyes on the man, Susan saw him glance up and down the road, then walk toward the steps leading up to the gallery. Smoothing the skirt of her cotton print dress, she took a deep breath, straightened her back, and walked over to the door. She opened it just as the man placed one boot up on the gallery.

"Good morning. Is there something I can do for you?" Susan asked. She saw that he had not been expecting her abrupt greeting, but he made the adjustment adeptly.

"Hi. I didn't know if there was anybody at home or not." He spoke with a raspy softness in his voice like sandpaper across smooth wood. Harshness seemed to lie just beneath the surface, straining to break through. "I hope I'm not interrupting anything important."

Susan felt the bothersome chill again. "Just a little housework. Nothing that can't wait." She watched the slow smile creep across his face. His white teeth and hair and pale eyes made her think of the skull that lay just beneath his taut skin. She offered politely, "Is there something I can do for you?"

He glanced around at the shed and the dock. Tied to a piling with a grass rope, the pirogue rocked slowly in the gentle waves slapping against its sides. "This sure is a nice place you got here. You out here all by yourself?"

"No!" Susan realized that she shouldn't have blurted the word out so defensively, but it was too late to take it back. "My husband and I live here." She tried to sound casual as she continued, holding the man's gaze. "He's a deputy with the sheriff's office — detective division."

"I'm sure he's a good one." The man stood still with one of his huge wide boots on the steps, the other on the gallery floor. Then he lifted the back foot and started across the gallery toward her. "How's the fishing around here?"

Susan shrugged. "I'm afraid you'll have to ask my husband about that." She continued to stare into the washed-out turquoise eyes. "He should be home any minute now."

"Would you like to buy some shrimp?"

"What?"

"Shrimp. You know — those little curved creatures with long feelers," he placed the knuckles of his forefingers on each side of his head and wriggled the fingers, "that live out in the Gulf. Wanna buy some? I'm selling them out of an ice chest in my truck. Give you a real good price."

"I . . . don't," taken off guard by the man's sudden change of direction, Susan seemed hardly able to answer the simple question. "I mean . . . no." She collected herself. "There's a man who lives down the road —

a fisherman. We buy most of our seafood from him. He's got a big family."

"I don't."

"Don't what?"

"Have a family." The man now stood three feet from Susan, towering over her. "None at all — just me. My mama never did care much about me."

"I'm sorry."

"Don't be." His lips curved back slowly over his white teeth. "She's dead."

Although his attitude was ominous, threatening, Susan suddenly felt a heavy sadness for this strange man with his over-worked muscles and his underfed soul. His eyes seemed devoid of emotion as though someone had pulled a plug somewhere inside of him long ago and drained it all away. "I think you've had a very hard life."

Now it was the big man's turn to be taken aback. He blinked his eyes as though ridding them of foreign particles, then turned them back on Susan. "Can I use your phone? My truck ain't running so good."

Through the screen door, the whistle of the teakettle broke the tension of his question. Susan knew that if he meant her harm, he would have no less trouble right here on the gallery than he would inside the cabin. "Come on in." She opened the door and motioned for him to follow her inside.

Inside the cabin she turned the burner off and pointed to the yellow wall phone next to the refrigerator. "You'll have to ring the operator if it's not a local call."

"It's local." His eyes took in the kitchen and living room through an open archway, then he glanced at Susan's open Bible on the table. He twisted his neck from side to side and rolled his shoulders as though warding off the cramps. "What'cha reading that thing for?"

"I like it."

"Oh." He walked over to the telephone, picked up the receiver, and hiding his motions from Susan, dialed his number.

Susan noticed that he had only dialed six numbers.

He held it to his ear for a count of six rings even though no number had been connected. "Well, I guess he ain't at his shop. Probably a road call."

"Can I offer you something to drink?" Susan asked. Somehow she knew that he would be leaving now.

The big man seemed to fill the kitchen as he stood near the refrigerator, his hand still holding to the receiver he had placed into its cradle. He turned the telephone loose and scratched his left ear, staring at Susan, seeing her for the first time. "No — no thanks. I gotta be going."

Susan opened the door for him. He still appeared confused and uneasy as he gave her a final look, brushing by her on the way out to the gallery.

Closing the door and locking it behind him, Susan leaned back against the door, took a deep breath and said, "Thank the Lord *that's* over!" She hurried to the window, pulled the curtain aside, and watched him get into his truck. The engine started like he had just driven it out of the showroom. Backing a short way down the gradual slope that led to the bayou, the man turned around and headed back in the direction he had come from. Susan noticed that there was no ice chest in the back of his truck.

Dylan, nursing his fifth cup of coffee, sat at a table at the far side of the Cafe du Monde's patio area closest to the river. From his position he could look straight down St. Ann Street, commanding a view of the entrance to the Pontalba Apartment building. He wore Levi's, boots, and a loose-fitting black shirt with its long tails hanging out, concealing Emile's .45 that nestled inside his waistband at the small of his back.

"Will there be anything else, sir?" The obviously impatient waiter, his smile growing progressively thinner each time he brought Dylan a refill, gazed down at him through Coke-bottle glasses. In his early twenties, he wore a small inner tube of fat around his waist beneath his starched white shirt, testifying to his own fondness for the beignets he served his customers.

Dylan glanced around the inner tube and down St. Ann Street. "Yes there is." He gave the man a benign smile. "You see the entrance to the Pontalba over there?"

The waiter gave him a skeptical look, then glanced over his shoulder. "Yes sir. It's been right there in the same place for a long time."

"I know you're busy, but would you mind keeping an eye on it for about two minutes?"

The waiter merely scowled his disapproval of his customer's unusual request.

Digging into his front pocket, Dylan pulled out a five-dollar bill and dropped it on the table. "You see, I have to go to the bathroom, and I'm waiting for someone to leave her apartment."

The scowl brightened at the sight of the bill, then grew dark again at Dylan's request.

"All you have to do is come get me if she leaves. What do you say?"

"What's she look like?" He placed his hand

on the bill, slid it across the table, and tucked it inside his front pocket.

Dylan gave him a brief description of Dianna and hurried off toward the men's room. When he returned the waiter was busying himself wiping the spotless table from the backside so he could watch the Pontalba's entrance. As soon as he saw Dylan, he picked up his tray and walked around the table. Glancing around, he said, "I'm glad you're back. One more cleaning and I believe that old table top might have caved right in."

"I appreciate this," Dylan said, pulling out his chair.

"More coffee?"

"I might as —" Dylan stopped in mid-sentence, his eyes fixed on a red Ford pickup turning onto St. Ann Street. "No, never mind. Thanks for your help."

"Sure thing. You come back now," the waiter said, watching Dylan thread his way between the tables, waiters, and customers on the crowded patio.

As Dylan reached Decatur Street, he saw Dianna hurry out the door of the apartment building in the glow of a streetlamp. She wore a short black dress and high heels and carried a bag across her shoulder. Hurrying across the street to his car, he watched her jerk open the door of the pickup and slide up onto the seat. Before the door had completely closed, the truck lurched forward.

Dylan jumped into the Volkswagen, started it, jammed the gearshift into first, and eased around the corner, following the red truck down St. Ann. Dylan tried to stay two or three cars back from the Ford. *Why aren't they using that blue Super Sport? If they are up to something, that red pickup won't make much of a getaway vehicle — it's too slow and too easy to spot.*

The truck stopped for the red light at the wide, bustling intersection of Canal. One of the old iron streetcars, looking like a misplaced twenties snapshot dropped into the seventies, whined around the far corner and headed down St. Charles. When the light changed, the Ford followed it, and Dylan followed the Ford — on past Gravier, Poydras, Lafayette, St. Joseph, and around Lee Circle with its granite statue of the general standing high on his pedestal surveying the city, then on through the Garden District.

Dylan kept the truck in sight in the four-lane traffic of St. Charles with the streetcar humming along on his left. The streetcar stopped and discharged passengers from its amber-lighted interior, and he caught up with another one further down the avenue. Turning right on General Pershing, the Ford drove several more blocks, turned right, then took a quick left and pulled over on a side street beneath the murky shadows of an ancient magnolia.

Dylan switched his headlights off, pulling onto a grassy area between the street and the sidewalk, partially shielded on one side by a tall hedge. The houses on both sides were dark. The blue-white light from a television glowed faintly in a window of the one closest to where he had parked.

Turning off the ignition, Dylan eased his door open, got out, and closed it quietly. Then he crossed the sidewalk, slipping along in the shadows of a row of cedars growing in the front yard of the corner house. As he reached the street corner, shielded by another hedge, he peered down the side street, murky in the faint light filtering down from the street lamp on the opposite corner.

The red pickup, lights turned off, was tilted sideways, both right tires resting in a shallow drainage ditch. Dylan watched it for a long two minutes, then the driver's side door opened and Dianna got out. She now wore black tennis shoes with her sleek outfit. In the anemic light, he saw her holding a slim metallic-looking object.

Dylan watched her trot smoothly across the street, turning right on the sidewalk toward a two-story stucco apartment building at the end of the short block. Its rear parking lot, bordered along the back by a three-foot board fence, held several cars.

Keeping his eye on the driver's door of the pickup, Dylan searched for a route to the apartment building that would avoid Teague. This side of the street would send him right by the pickup. He decided that his only option would be to cross the street at the corner, run past the first house, and cut through the side yard, coming up on the opposite side of the parking lot from the side Dianna was entering.

He saw Dianna stop at the entrance to the lot, turn and wave toward the truck, then she walked deliberately in toward the parked cars. Thinking that Teague would be looking in the opposite direction, Dylan leaned from the waist and sprinted across the street to the corner, diving behind a huge spreading gardenia bush. He was up immediately, glanced at the pickup — no movement there — then ran across the front yard and down the side yard of the white frame house.

At the corner of the back lot he stopped, kneeling down behind the board fence of the parking lot. He saw Dianna standing next to a red Corvette. She appeared to be making an adjustment to a long slim rod, glinting silver in the light shining from one of the apartment windows. Using two hands, she lifted the tip of the metal rod above the car's window, slipping it down inside the window to begin working it slowly up and down.

Dylan felt the warm night breeze against the back of his neck, carrying the fragrance of the gardenias growing in the backyard he had just crossed. From one of the windows in the apartment building, a tinny radio played Bobby Goldsboro's syrupy sweet hit, "Honey."

Without warning, Dianna let go of her burglary tool, turning deliberately around to face him. He thought she must have heard something, then realized that he couldn't have made any sound that would have carried that far. She stared directly at him, although he knew that he was not visible to her.

Instantly a cold stab of fear gripped Dylan's chest. His right hand had only moved six inches toward the .45 in his waistband when a searing pain shot through his right temple. Broken shards of red and yellow and white light exploded inside his head, each piercing his skull as they exited into the darkness. Then he felt himself rushing downward inside a cold, narrow well toward the center of the earth.

Listen to the music playing in your head. Dylan wondered how the Beatles and all their musical equipment could have gotten down into the well with him. Forcing his way upward out of a clutching darkness, he could feel his own heart beating, but somehow it no longer rested in his chest; someone had transplanted it beneath the skin of his right temple.

Lying on his back next to the fence where he had fallen, he felt the .45's hard and reassuring pressure against his spine. As he struggled to sit up, he discovered that the music was playing from somewhere in the apartment building across the quiet parking lot. Then he realized, gingerly lifting his hand to the side of his head, that the lump just above his temple was the source of the throbbing heartbeat.

Dylan sat next to the fence trying to reconstruct what had happened to him. It came back fuzzy and distorted: the red truck reeling ahead of him in the amber light of St. Charles with streetcars rattling alongside the Volkswagen; then the darkened streets and houses; running in the open with his eye on the pickup — That was it! Teague had already left the truck and lay in wait for him in one of a dozen hiding places somewhere out in the murky darkness.

Then Dianna stood again next to the Corvette, giving him that casual glance, secure in the knowledge that everything was still under her control. He could almost see in the glow of the apartment windows the faint beginnings of that haughty smile.

Feeling that his head would surely shatter with any slight jarring, Dylan placed his right hand against his temple, cradling it against his palm as he grabbed the fence with his left hand and struggled to his feet. The night had that 3:00 A.M. feeling, dead and dry and empty, as though the city was holding its breath, longing for one more sunrise.

Returning to his car by the same route that had taken him to its abrupt and painful end, Dylan climbed inside, lay his head back against the seat, and waited for the two streetlights on the pole at the end of the block to become one. Gradually they wavered back and forth, then finally blended into a single yellow-white glow.

An orange cat, its tail moving slowly from side to side like a long bushy rudder, padded softly along the sidewalk toward the Volkswagen. Dylan watched it react to some sound unheard by him, then slip sideways and disappear as though the shadows had swallowed it.

Sometime later Dylan blinked his eyes, realizing that he had dozed off or lost consciousness; it bothered him that he could not tell which. After digging his keys out of his front pocket, he started the engine and drove back through the almost deserted streets to the grocery, parked on a side street, and climbed the stairs to his apartment.

Inside he took off his shirt and boots, cracked a half tray of ice into a towel and, grabbing a pillow off the bed, walked into the living room. He opened the French doors. The breeze off the river felt cool on his bare skin.

Then he stretched out on the couch, pulled the pillow beneath his head, and placed the ice-filled towel against his temple. The pillowcase felt comforting against the back of his head, the ice cool and soothing against his throbbing temple. Off in the distance, a dog barked twice.

Afterglow filled the room like a lavender mist; a thin line of clouds, their edges tinted with peach-colored light, streaked the sky out beyond the open door. Dylan felt cool dampness against his head from the melted ice. He lifted his head from the wet pillow and eased up on one elbow. At first he thought sunrise was at hand; then the sounds out in the streets told him that he had slept the day through and it was twilight.

Sliding his legs off the couch, he sat with his head in his hands, breathing deeply, feeling dizzy and weak and slightly nauseous. After a few minutes, he felt some strength return. He reached for the phone on the table next to the couch, picked up the receiver, and dialed home. After one ring, Susan answered.

"Hello."

"Hi. It's me."

"Dylan —" Susan's voice sounded fragile, as though she had willed herself to keep her anxiety at bay. "I was *so* worried. Why didn't you call?"

Dylan listened to the sounds of laughter drifting up from the street. "I got tied up trying to get a lead on this case and just now had time to call."

Susan let her breath out slowly. "That's what I told myself. I forget sometimes that your work isn't like teaching school. I always knew where I'd be and when."

"Nothing to worry about." Dylan reached for the wet towel next to him, placing it against the warm pulse of his temple. "I'll try to get home in a day or two."

"Are you sleeping enough?"

Dylan smiled. "I sure am."

"How about eating? You're not just shoveling down a bunch of junk food, are you?"

At the sound of Susan's words, Dylan noticed an empty gnawing feeling in his stomach and tried to remember the last time he had eaten. *Beignets last night with all that coffee.* "I'm doing all right. If I've got to be away from home, New Orleans is the place for good food."

"I know what's down there, Dylan. It's where I grew up, remember?" She sounded impatient, almost irritable. "I just want to make sure you're eating some of it . . . and something that's reasonably healthy for you."

"I think I'll go out and order something special then. A spinach soufflé and some celery shish kebab." Hearing a conspicuous absence of laughter on Susan's end of the line, Dylan changed the subject to what was really on his mind. "How's the baby?"

"Sleeping, thank goodness!" Now Susan was the one who sounded a little weary. "Sometimes I think he's playing a tennis match in there . . . or riding a pony."

"Did you say *he?*"

"When it's active it's a *he;* when it's quiet it's a *she.*"

"How's Emile?" he asked, inquiring about his friend and colleague.

"Ornery as ever. Emma's fussing over him like an old hen, but he won't slow down."

"Anything interesting going on?"

"We had a missionary from Brazil speak at church. Her husband was killed by the Indians down there, but she stayed on to finish his work . . . and she's going back in two months. That was kind of interesting."

Dylan thought that he never would understand that kind of dedication and sacrifice. "Anything else?"

After a brief silence, Susan said, "Nothing much. A man came by selling shrimp, but I told him we already had somebody we buy from."

Dylan pictured the idyllic setting of the cabin on the quiet bayou at the edge of the great Basin. "Sounds like you're having a real wild time up there."

"Emmaline and I went up to Baton Rouge to the movie and saw *Love Story*."

"How was it?"

"Kind of sappy."

"I could have told you that, if it was anything at all like the book. Eric Segal's the Rod McKuen of novelists." He turned the towel around, pressing the cool side to his temple. "I think I'm beginning to miss you, Susan St. John."

"I should hope so!"

"I always liked the sound of that — Susan St. John. Has a nice ring to it, don't you think?"

"I think so." After a brief silence, she said, "You be sure and get home in a day or two, Dylan."

"I will. Call Emile or Emma if you need anything."

"You be careful. I love you, Dylan."

"I loved you first."

"You did *not!* You didn't have sense enough to love me when we first met."

"No, I definitely loved you first, Susan." Dylan knew he had caught her off guard. "You had too many boyfriends to love anybody."

"You should be ashamed of yourself, talking about the mother of your child like this!"

Dylan smiled, knowing he had won this newest word game. "I'm absolutely delirious with shame."

"You are not! You think it's funny sneaking up on me like that, don't you?"

Feeling a heavy weariness weigh down on him, even though he had slept the day away, Dylan said, "Guess I'd better get off this phone and get some sleep."

"Good-night then. Love you."

"You too." Dylan felt drowsy and slightly nauseous. He stood up shakily, holding to the edge of the sofa for balance. Outside, the year-long French Quarter party was cranking up for another night. He eased the French doors closed, cutting out most of the noise. Then he went into the kitchen and drank two glasses of ice water, got a fresh towel from the bathroom, and dumped the remainder of the ice tray into it.

Walking as though he was on his way to a nursing home crafts class, he took his icy towel and a third glass of water into the living room and sat down on the couch. He turned the damp pillow over to its dry side, then thought about trying to find a plastic bag to cover the towel. He decided it was too much trouble and stretched out, placing the towel against the side of his head.

Lying with his head elevated by the couch's armrest, he suddenly felt the nausea leave him. The drone of the Quarter hovered outside the door, but in the quiet darkness of the apartment he felt like a fox safely in its lair after eluding the pack. He let himself slip down, down into a quiet place, his head resting in Susan's lap while her soft hand caressed his face and the side of his head, easing the throbbing pain.

11

Barataria

Birds chirping outside on the balcony awakened Dylan. He carefully opened his eyes to a rosy pink light filtering in through the window panes. His head felt full of cobwebs, but the throbbing pain had drained away into the wet pillowcase. The lump on his head had almost gone away, but was still tender to the touch. He lay there watching the light change colors. When it showed a tinge of pale gold, he sat up. No dizziness. He walked into the kitchen and drank a glass of water from the tap.

Feeling that his strength had returned, Dylan took a shower, shaved, brushed the crusty feeling from his teeth, and combed his wet hair. Then he put on clean Levi's, his boots, and a blue plaid shirt. After taking another glass of water out on the balcony and drinking it while he sat in the porch swing, he decided that he was ready to face another day.

Downstairs in the grocery, he saw Romano at the far end of the counter pouring his first cup of coffee from a white enamel French drip pot. *He actually does leave that stool.* "Morning, Mr. Romano. Things going to suit you?"

"Too early to tell," Romano remarked as he stirred sugar into the black steaming coffee. Then he carried the white mug back to his stool. He motioned for Dylan to help himself to coffee. "What'd you find out yesterday?"

"Yesterday?" Dylan walked over, poured coffee, and dumped in a spoon of sugar.

"Certainly." Romano slurped the hot coffee. "I figured you was working on it all day."

Confused, Dylan walked back to the counter. "I'm afraid you've lost me."

"You don't know?"

Dylan shrugged. "I've been a little under the weather. Slept most of yesterday."

Romano dropped the *Times Picayune* on the counter. "It made the *States Item* yesterday afternoon; the *Picayune* this morning."

Dylan gazed in disbelief at the headlines, an icy blade of fear twisting inside his chest. FOURTH MAYOR SLAIN, and in smaller letters, KILLER USES MACE. "A mace this time."

"I thought that was kinda funny, too," Romano said. "I thought cops sprayed that stuff out of a can."

"It's not that kind of mace," Dylan said absently, his eyes still riveted on the newspaper. "It's a weapon that was used by knights in medieval times."

"Well, I don't have time to read much more than the headlines usually." Romano slurped his coffee as he gazed at the upside-down newspaper. "Dead is dead, though — don't much matter if it comes out of a can or a gun barrel." He reached beneath the counter and handed Dylan three slips of paper. "I didn't see your car so I didn't bother coming up to see if you was home."

"I parked around the corner." Dylan took the slips, seeing that Emile had called three times yesterday. "You mind if I use your telephone?"

Romano reached beneath the counter and placed the heavy black telephone in front of Dylan. "Help yourself. Emile told me to keep up with the charges and the sheriff's department would reimburse me."

Dylan dialed the number and waited for two rings. "Elaine . . . Yeah, I know . . . Is he there? . . . Okay." Dylan took a yellow pencil from an empty Campbell's Tomato Soup can and began tapping the eraser on the Formica counter.

"Emile . . . Yeah, I know, I'll tell you about it later. . . . All right . . . I'll go on down to Barataria and see what I can find out, then come up there when I'm finished. . . . You'll tell Susan . . . Everything's going all right. . . . Okay. See you then." He hung the phone up and shoved it across the counter to Romano.

Returning the telephone to its shelf, Romano said, "Some mayor sure must have done some bad stuff to this fella."

Stunned and distracted, Dylan skimmed through the body of the article. "Who?"

"The killer — that's who. Why else would he be killing nobody but mayors?"

Dylan nodded, folding the newspaper and handing it back to Romano. "I think you're right."

Jean Lafitte and his pirates loved the dark, isolated bayous and backwaters of Barataria and its virgin stands of cypress towering above the swamps and massive live oaks strung with delicate silver-gray strands of Spanish moss. Then came the hunters, fishermen, trappers, and loggers to settle in these lands. They built their homes on elevated sites next to the bayous, the Indian middens or shell banks scattered throughout the marsh. Some constructed their homes on pilings driven into the swamp to make them convenient to their work.

These settlers traveled this sometimes dark and forbidding land by pirogues — fragile, narrow boats made from hollowed-out cypress logs. Their towns were built along the water courses. Barataria was one of the first of these elongated cities known as line settlements.

Dylan parked his car behind a battered forties-vintage Ford pickup and waited for the ferry. A hunched-over man in a straw hat sat behind the steering wheel, yelling at his unfortunate dark-haired son to get his head back inside the window.

Wiping the sweat off his forehead with the back of his hand, Dylan glanced out both windows. He turned off his engine, got out, and walked over to a stand of black gum trees and sat down in the shade. The long, cool grass looked inviting. Lying on his back, he stared up at a few scattered wisps of clouds sailing across the blue sky.

"Hey, you!"

Dylan raised his head, staring at the man in the straw hat whose head was sticking out the window of his truck.

"You better get you'self over here if you wanna ketch dat ferry!" He yelled as though Dylan was a quarter-mile away instead of only twenty yards.

Glancing at the short barge used to ferry cars and light trucks, Dylan saw that it had just left the opposite shore. He lay his head back down for another minute, then got up and walked slowly back to his car. "Plenty of time," he said softly to the man, whose head was still hanging out the window. The boy was now standing on the window ledge peering over the top of the pickup.

As Dylan climbed back inside the Volkswagen, he saw the boy suddenly snatched back inside.

A short ferry ride and a half-mile drive later, Dylan pulled off the road and parked in the shade of a sycamore tree. Getting out of the car, he walked across in the white glare of the oyster-shell road toward a small clapboard grocery. Nugrape, RC Cola, Camel cigarettes, and a varied assortment of other advertisements made from tin rectangles covered the front of the store. A single red gas pump stood out front like a squat and bulky gunfighter packing its pistol in a groove at its side.

A tiny building made of white-painted plywood and attached to the right side of the grocery was marked in bold block letters *U.S. Post Office, Barataria, Louisiana*. Its doorway led out onto the narrow gallery running the length of the grocery. Its twin on the left proclaimed in the same black lettering that it was home to the *Barataria Police Department.*

Turning left on the gallery, Dylan opened the screen door hanging on two of its three hinges, and stepped inside. The chubby man sleeping in his chair behind the old gray metal desk wore matching, but wrinkled, dark blue shirt and trousers, black cowboy boots, and a *Red Man* baseball cap. A brown and gray mat of stubble grew around and outward from his opened mouth.

A cane-bottomed chair sat in front of the desk, a green filing cabinet with two of its four drawers half-opened occupied the far corner of the room, and a paintless table holding five assorted mugs and a single-burner hotplate with an aluminum coffee pot rested against the opposite wall. A NAPA calendar tacked to the wall pictured a lithe blonde in cut-off jeans leaning over the fender and beneath the opened hood of a late-model Chevy pickup. She grasped a huge, spotless crescent wrench in her manicured hand.

Dylan turned back toward the sleeper, trying to decide whether to wake him or leave a note in his mouth and come back later. Suddenly, with a snorting, sputtering outrush of breath and a spasmodic jerking of his squat body, the man fell out of his chair, landing with a heavy thud on the bare wood floor.

Stepping around the desk, Dylan knelt down and asked, "Are you all right?"

The man sat up, knuckling the sleep from his eyes. "Mais yeah," he said, grinning at Dylan. "I gotta lot of padding, me. Didn't hurt nuttin'."

Dylan stuck out his hand, helping the man to his feet. "Dylan St. John. I didn't mean to wake you."

"Ray Daigle. Pleased to meet you." Daigle righted his chair and plopped down in it, motioning for Dylan to take the other one. "Nah, you didn't wake me up, no. I had me a night —" he stopped and grinned, "it couldn't be a nightmare 'cause it's still day-time, so I guess I just had a bad dream." He rubbed his eyes again and yawned. "It ain't no wonder though, after what I seen night before last."

"What was that?"

Daigle gave him a suspicious look, scratching his stubbled face with nails gnawed down to the fingertips.

"Sorry," Dylan said, reaching into his back pocket. He showed Daigle his badge and the commission that identified him as a member of the governor's task force.

"You kinda late, you."

"What do mean?"

"This place was buzzing like a kicked hornet's nest all day yesterday and half the night . . . State Police, cops out of New Orleans, some of your task force buddies." Daigle folded his hands on his ample stomach. "Last time I seen that many guns, I was sittin' in a John Wayne movie."

"Can you tell me what happened?"

Daigle made a face, then rubbed it away with both hands. "It wudn't purty, no." He shook his head slowly from side to side. "Poor ol' T-rass."

"Who's that?"

"The mayor." Daigle stared in disbelief at Dylan. He obviously thought him mired in ignorance. "Everybody knows T-rass. He been down here so long some people say he taught Jean Lafitte how to sail a boat."

"Does he have another name?"

Daigle pondered the question. "Mendoza. Rex Mendoza. He got that name T-rass a long time ago. One night, anyhow, this is how the story goes —"

"I'd like to get to the part about what you saw if that's all right."

The hurt look in Daigle's eyes lasted only seconds as though Dylan was not the first person lacking the civility to appreciate a good anecdote. "Well, I tole my story a dozen times already. One more won't hurt, I guess." He frowned at Dylan's relaxed posture. "Ain't you gonna take some notes, you?"

"I'll get a copy of the full report out of Baton Rouge. Just tell me what you remember." Dylan listened to Daigle relate his comings and goings the night of the murder. His description of Mendoza's head injury was appallingly graphic. When he finished, Dylan asked, "That's all you remember?"

"Yep." A bemused expression crawled onto Daigle's round, stubbled face.

"Something else?"

"Not really," he said, glancing at the floor. "It's just that my mind might not have been exactly on my work that night . . . not as good as usual, that is."

"Why not?"

"Well, I didn't tell none of them other cops. With all their fancy suits and big cars and stuff, they might think I'm just a hick police chief. It wasn't nothin' to do with the case anyhow. But," he glanced at Dylan as though at a kindred spirit, "you look kinda like I do. You know, not puttin' on airs and stuff like that."

Dylan nodded his agreement.

"Anyhow, I finished my rounds on the other side of the bayou and was waitin' for the ferry to cross back over here. Must of been close to midnight 'cause that's when it stops running and I barely made the last crossing." A smile lazed across Daigle's face. "That's when I seen her."

"Her?"

"And I mean *her*."

Dylan leaned forward in his chair.

"First thing got my attention was that car. A Corvette — red and shiny as anything you ever saw."

Dylan's mind turned on the picture of Dianna standing next to the red Corvette two nights before.

"And when it come bumping off the ferry next to me," he took a deep breath and sighed like a school boy, "there she was! Prettiest thing you ever saw."

"Can you describe her?"

Daigle nodded, his eyes glassy with the memory. "She had on this lacy little dress, what I could see of it, and it didn't cover up much," he winked at Dylan, "if you know what I mean."

"What about her face?"

"Oh, yeah. Couldn't tell, but I bet it was just as pretty as the part I could see."

"You couldn't see her?"

"She had her head turned kinda away from me, and all this long dark hair was hanging down. I couldn't really tell what she looked like."

"Anything else you can tell me?"

Daigle shook his head. "Anyhow, my thinkin' was kinda fuzzy for a while after that." He stared at the brightness of the single window. "A man just don't see a woman like that every day of his life . . . especially down here."

"Thanks for your help." Dylan stood up and walked toward the rickety screen door.

"Sorry I couldn't tell you more." Daigle leaned back in his chair, his eyelids already drooping toward sleep. "Y'all better ketch dis man real soon. He's a mean one."

Dylan nodded and walked out into the bright, warm June morning.

"It's her, Emile. I'm absolutely certain now."

"Not much doubt about it," Emile agreed. He sat behind his desk, the stack of reports in front of him freshly Xeroxed and stapled neatly together. "But you see this," he nodded toward the reports, "the latest from the task force. And they don't give us even one fact that connects any murder to Dianna Salazar or that trained gorilla, Teague, that she keeps on her leash." .

Dylan had turned every fact and lead inside out, including his own personal contacts, and could come up with no chain of evidence leading to Dianna. Not one eyewitness, not one piece of hard evidence. "There's got to be some way we can nail her." His voice was freighted with weariness and frustration. "She thinks the law can't touch her."

"So far she's been right," Emile admitted. He picked up the stack of reports and dumped them into his open file drawer. "Well, these things are useless. You told me more in ten minutes than I learned in days of digging in that pile of bureaucratic trash."

"What do we do next?"

"Your guess is as good as mine."

Dylan gazed through the tall window at the afternoon breeze, lifting strands of moss in the live oaks. The pale sunlight turned silver when it hit the delicate gray tendrils. "I've got to go back to New Orleans."

"Are you *nuts?*" Emile sat up in his chair. "She's *on* to you now!"

"Doesn't matter."

"What do you *mean*, it doesn't matter?" Emile's voice rose in pitch. "It means that she and that big goon might not give you a second chance."

"I think she's known all along."

"Known that you're a cop?"

Dylan nodded. "I can't prove it." He turned back toward Emile, his gaze level. "Just like I can't prove she killed those men. But I *know* it."

Emile stared at the floor, his head shaking slowly back and forth, then he lifted his head part-way up, seemingly unable to face Dylan square on as he spoke. "I hate to admit it, but you're the best hope we've got."

"I'll spend the night at home and go back in the morning," Dylan said. He slumped against the side of Emile's desk, folding his arms across his chest. "I need a night with my wife, in my own bed, away from that . . . city."

"Susan needs it more than you, I think."

Dylan stood up, rubbing the back of his neck. Weariness seemed to clutch at him like a clawed creature. Deeper than physical tiredness, it warred against his soul. "I've got to finish this quick so I can come home for good." He felt somehow that he needed Susan even more than she needed him, although he could not have stated why in words.

"You don't have to go back."

Dylan felt he didn't want to waste the energy to respond.

"You don't have to go back," Emile said again.

Dylan turned and walked toward the door, calling back over his shoulder, "Yes I do."

Emile opened his middle desk drawer, took out two keys on a metal ring, and tossed them over to Dylan. "Take the Blazer then. You're in the open now anyway, and you just might need something more substantial than that Bug. I'll have somebody drive it out to your house tomorrow."

"Okay." Dylan laid the key to his Volkswagen on the desk. "See you in a couple of days."

Dylan raised up on one elbow, resting his side against the pillow. He gazed out the window at the light-rimmed eastern sky, glowing like a bed of embers. It reminded him of the campfire of his first long-ago hunt with his father. Afterwards they sat together next to the fire wrapped in a blanket until the fear and exhilaration and sadness inside became a drowsy, comfortable warmth.

Next to him, the sound of Susan's soft, slow breathing gave him a feeling of comfort and ease. Softly brushing her hair back from her face with the backs of his fingers, he thought back on those early days of their marriage: *Susan stood at the stove in the high-*

ceilinged kitchen of their first apartment, with early sunlight streaming through the bank of windows over the sink, and him, slouched at the table, muscles aching and brain addled from some whirlwind road trip to Knoxville or Athens or Austin. Sipping strong black coffee, he watched her move about the kitchen, barefoot and wearing a faded sweatshirt with "LSU TENNIS" on the back and flour sprinkles on the front, bewildered by his good fortune.

Quietly opening the drawer of the nightstand, Dylan took out a legal pad and a number two pencil. Placing the pad on the bed, he lay on his side, his back to Susan. The sunrise cast faint light on his writing tablet. Quiet memories of other early mornings in bed with Susan drifted through his mind as he wrote:

> I remember cool, quiet morning
>   hours most
> Rose-colored light and drowsy mist
> Sweet innocence of your sleeping
> There never seemed time enough
> Just to look at you
> In dreams a child . . . awaking
> To give a woman's warm embrace

Dylan felt the bed move behind him. Susan's warm, soft hand slipped along his side, resting on his stomach. She spoke in a voice still thick with sleep. "What are you doing awake at this time of the morning?"

"Just scratching down a few lines," he answered, laying the pad aside and turning over to face her. "I might try to do something with them later."

"Poetry?"

"Not yet, but maybe if I work on it awhile."

Susan sat up in bed, smoothing her hair back with both hands. "Let me see."

"I told you it's just a few scratchings. Give me some time to do something with it first."

"I *like* scratchings." Susan held out her hand, her green eyes clear and shining in the light from the sun lifting now through the seam between the earth and the sky.

Dylan reached behind him and handed her the tablet, then stretched out on the bed, hands behind his head, watching the play of light across the ceiling.

In a few moments Susan curled next to him, her hand flat against his chest, her head resting in the hollow of his shoulder. Her fingers traced intricate patterns on his skin. "Did I really look like a child back then?"

"You still do."

"It did seem like there was never enough

time . . . to, I don't know . . . just be to-gether."

"Maybe if we had had all the time we wanted . . . then those times together wouldn't seem so . . . so *dear* to us now. Maybe we wouldn't treasure them so much."

"That's awfully philosophical for so early in the morning, don't you think?"

Dylan cupped his left hand over the swell of her hip. "Hmmm . . ."

"Are you going back to sleep?"

"Heaven forbid."

"I think I'll join you then." She kissed him on the cheek, slipping her left hand inside his right and settling her head comfortably against his shoulder.

"Only if you let me take the journey with you through your dreams."

"Hmmm."

Dylan let go of the world then, feeling Susan soft and warm against him, the caress of her breath on his neck, and he drifted down, down into an enfolding, dreamless dark.

12

The Knife

Dylan stood behind Damon Carbelli's desk, surveying the framed certificates that covered most of the back wall of his office. The FBI, the local Lion's Club, the Boy Scouts of America, the Louisiana Peace Officer's Association, and dozens of other organizations had seen fit to reward Carbelli for his diligence to improving himself in his chosen profession or for his unselfish devotion to his fellow man.

Walking around the desk, Dylan noticed that it was spotless and orderly, the framed family portrait, name plate, and office memorabilia in neat geometric arrangement. The tile floor gleamed like polished marble and the two burgundy-covered mahogany chairs sat at right angles exactly in line with opposite edges of the desk.

Dylan sat down in the right-hand chair and waited as he had been instructed by Carbelli's young, blonde, and fashionably dressed secretary.

The door opened and in he came, walking as if he were being graded by headquarters staff in a full-dress parade. He wore a tailored, dark brown, pinstripe suit with a shirt so white it almost hurt to look at it. The brown-and-tan striped necktie was studiously shaped in a Windsor knot. His lean cheeks gleamed as though he had just shaved.

"Sorry to keep you waiting," he said with absolutely no conviction in his voice.

Dylan rose to shake his hand, but Carbelli ignored or failed to see the gesture. Dylan stood there a few seconds with his hand sticking out like a friendly mannequin while Carbelli busied himself tidying up a neat stack of correspondence.

"Now, what can I do for you?" Carbelli asked through gleaming teeth that spoke of rigorous and faithful brushing and flossing.

Dylan grabbed the arms of the chair with both hands and slid it three inches to the right. He managed not to smile when he saw Carbelli flinch. "I've been shuffled around so much by the New Orleans Police Department today, I've almost forgotten what I wanted to see you about."

"Well," Carbelli said by way of explanation, "you know how bureaucracies function."

"Dysfunction."

"What?"

"Bureaucracies *dysfunction* more than they function," Dylan corrected. He eased the chair another inch to the right. "At least that's been *my* experience."

Carbelli quickly replaced his blank expression with one of benign tolerance. "Yes, well I'm sure that's all well and good, but that doesn't tell me why you wanted to see me today." He frowned as he inspected the tieless open collar of Dylan's slightly wrinkled white shirt.

Dylan realized then that Carbelli already knew precisely why he had come to see him and had known since shortly after Dylan had explained his reasons at ten o'clock that morning downtown at the chief's office. The grizzled old sergeant, who was the only person he had been allowed to speak to, had sent him on a bumper-pool route around town, ending at the district office on Rampart Street at the edge of the Quarter.

"It's about Dianna Salazar," Dylan clarified.

Carbelli nodded and smiled as though Dylan had just invoked the name of his favorite saint. "I've known Sunny since she was just a little girl."

Maybe I'd better just forget the whole thing and get out of here, Dylan thought. He pushed the idea aside, took heart, and launched into his story, trying to make his case against Dianna "Sunny" Salazar sound convincing.

Carbelli listened with condescension. He scowled fiercely once or twice when Dylan's narrative hit a particularly graphic note in the sequence of events that had led him to this office. When Dylan finished, Carbelli rested his elbows on his desk, folding his hands together under his chin. "Now, let's see if I understand you."

He stared at something above Dylan's head as he spoke. "There isn't *one* piece of evidence, not one single witness that places Sunny at any of the crime scenes. She has no apparent motive for any of the murders, and she has never," he lowered his eyes toward Dylan, "as far as we can ascertain, had even a passing contact with any of the victims."

He remained perfectly still as he continued to speak. "Am I correct so far?"

Dylan nodded, feeling that his first inclination to forget the whole thing had been the right one.

"However," Carbelli said as he stood up,

clasped his hands behind his back in the "at ease" position, and paced an abbreviated path back and forth behind his desk, "you saw a shadowy figure that you *can't* identify, running away after your mayor up in Evangeline was killed; you saw Sunny standing next to a red Corvette on the other side of the Garden District the night this last murder took place some forty miles away down in Barataria, and —"

Carbelli sat down again, shaking his head slowly back and forth. "She's a good shot with a crossbow." He arched his professionally dyed brows and finished, "Does *that* about sum up your story?"

"You left out the part about how weird her neighbors in the Quarter think she is."

Carbelli's laugh ended in a snort. "*Everybody* in the Quarter is weird. Some more than others." He rubbed his palms together slowly. "People my age think *most* of the young folks Dianna's age are weird. That doesn't make them killers."

"What about the burglary tool I saw her with?" Dylan asked. He was quickly realizing what the factual basis of his case would look like to a grand jury.

"Thirty — forty yards away . . . at night, and you can say for *sure* she was carrying a burglary tool?"

"Why don't you contact the owner of the Corvette?" Dylan suggested. He suddenly found himself on the defensive. "At least check the files to see if one was reported stolen that night."

"All that was done within two hours after you left the chief's office this morning." Carbelli's expression had gone beyond smug. "The owner said his automobile was exactly as he had left it the night before."

"That's easy enough to explain. They hot-wired it and brought it back the same night."

Carbelli stood up again, perched on the side of his desk, and hitched his trouser leg up so as not to flatten its knife-edge crease. "Mr. St. John . . ."

Dylan thought Carbelli made the name sound like some kind of infectious disease.

"I know that you're a member of the governor's task force and that it would be a real feather in the cap of *someone like you* to catch this 'Camelot Killer.' " Carbelli's face had worked itself into a smirk.

At the side of the chair, Dylan's hand balled into a fist. He saw himself taking one quick step toward Carbelli and driving his knuckles into the clean, shiny line of his jaw. Then he pictured himself spending the night in the New Orleans lockup and drove the thought from his mind.

"But I'm sure you'll have to agree that the district attorney would dismiss these allegations quicker than I would like for you to leave New Orleans," Carbelli said with finality.

Stunned by the impact of Carbelli's words, Dylan simply stared at him.

"You heard me correctly, Mr. St. John. I — or should I say *we* — would like you to leave our city as soon as you can check out of your hotel."

Dylan felt a sense of relief that the police didn't know where he was staying, which meant they probably didn't know how long he had been in town or what he had been doing except for the parts he had told them. He saw absolutely no hope of recourse with Carbelli or the powers that backed him. In fact, he saw no good reason to speak a single word more to Damon Carbelli, but he did. Standing up, he said, "Thanks for your time," and walked out the door.

The fragrance of Jungle Gardenia perfume hung in the still air. As Dylan stepped onto the landing at the top of the stairs outside his apartment door, he reached behind him and slipped the .45 out of his waistband. Jacking a round into the chamber, he flicked the safety off, gripped the doorknob, and slowly cracked the door. Standing to the right side, he peered around the door jamb with enough open space to see across the kitchen and directly through the living room to the open French doors.

Dianna, a slim wine glass in her right hand, stood on the balcony gazing down into the street. She wore a short black dress with lace at the hem, sheer black stockings, and black high-heels. Her dark hair fell across her bare shoulders.

Dylan shoved the safety on and slipped the automatic back inside his waistband. Then, as quietly as he could, he stepped into the kitchen.

"Hello, Dylan." Dianna turned slowly around, her smile that of a cat gazing at a cornered mouse. "I had no idea how long they'd keep giving you the run-around."

"*They?*"

"My father's people."

Dylan continued on into the living room, his right hand held loosely at his side. "You make it sound like the police are slaves and your father owns the plantation."

"Not quite." She stepped inside, taking a sip of the pale amber-colored wine. "A cop is a cop, after all. They checked out the information you gave them and decided it was useless." She smiled sweetly. "Then they called *me*. Or perhaps I should say that *Damon Carbelli* called me. I believe that was several hours before you got to his office."

"Why would he do that?"

"*Why?* For my own protection, of course."

"You lost me."

Sitting down on the sofa, Dianna crossed her legs. "The consensus is that you're a disturbed, possibly dangerous young man, Dylan."

"You've always had it your way, haven't you, Dianna? Daddy's little girl."

Sparks flared in her eyes, then settled to a glow. "Sit down, Dylan."

Dylan stood gazing down on her.

"Oh, come on," she said, patting the sofa next to her, that childish whine not quite concealed at the back of her voice. "Sit with me."

Dylan just looked at her and said nothing.

Dianna patted the couch again. "Let's not fight. Come sit next to me."

"I'm fine right here."

She drained the glass, placing it on the table next to the telephone, then tilted her head back and shook her hair out, smoothing it back into place with both hands. Then she looked into Dylan's eyes, smiling, and abruptly her eyes changed as though something had clicked into or out of place. They widened in mild surprise and shock. Her mouth softened, and she tilted her head to one side as though it had grown suddenly heavy. "Dylan," she said in a voice barely louder than a whisper.

She placed the toe of one shoe on the heel of the other and slipped out of it, then the other, curling her legs up beside her on the couch. "Please . . . at least sit down on the couch. I feel like a scolded child!"

Dylan braced himself against the strong pull into the walking, breathing emotional vortex named Dianna Salazar. "How did you know I was following you the other night?"

Dianna shook her head slowly, making a clicking sound against her teeth with the tip of her tongue. "You've led such a sheltered life, haven't you?"

"Humor me," he said flatly.

She smiled. "I enjoy you *so* very much!" Then she folded her hands primly on her lap. "You made quite an impression on me at the Evangeline Fair."

For the first time, Dylan was beginning to understand what had happened to him. He saw again the dark-clad figure running gracefully toward the bayou in the deep shade of a live oak. "You've lost me again."

"Two feet more to the left, and I'd have been dead."

He remembered the frosty patch of glass in the back window of the Super Sport where his bullet had shattered it.

Dianna continued as casually as if she had been telling about a recent trip to the supermarket. "Well, after that, I just had to find out who you were. I'm simply amazed at the information one can get on a person today with our police department's electronic marvels — if you have the proper contacts, of course. I may know more about *you* than you know about yourself.

"I was absolutely delighted when you showed up at the Camelot Festival," she continued. Her expression was that of a five-year-old about to blow out the candles on her birthday cake. "It's been *such* good fun!"

"Did *you* kill those men, or did you have your trained ape do it for you?"

Dianna ignored the question. "Every man I've ever known would have made a pass at me by now, sugar. The closest you've come is to call me a 'nice girl.' "

Dylan pictured Dianna in this very dress, alluring, seductive, making Jimmy Iverson forget about his plain little wife. He could see her, using all of her almost-childish charm to make him cross the line, then making him pay the ultimate price for his infidelity.

"I'm married, Dianna."

She looked as though Dylan had just betrayed her. Getting up from the couch, she snatched her glass from the table and walked in her stocking feet into the kitchen. Opening the refrigerator door, she took out the wine bottle and poured her glass full again, then took an identical glass from the kitchen table and filled it, too. "Here. You can at least have a glass of wine with me." She handed the glass to Dylan on her way back to her end of the couch.

"Men don't keep their vows," Dianna stated as she stared into glass. "There must be something *wrong* with you."

Dylan realized that his questions would never get him the answers he needed. He hoped that his silence would.

Dianna took a swallow of wine, then gave Dylan a long, hard stare. "*Is* there something wrong with you, Dylan St. John?"

Holding his glass of wine, Dylan returned her gaze, keeping his expression intentionally blank.

"I really *do* like you," Dianna said softly, then frowned at the noise drifting up from the street. "Isn't that strange? The only man who *isn't* interested in me, and I find *him*," she gave him a drowsy smile, "*deliciously* attractive."

"Dianna, this has got to stop."

"I can't help it if I find you attractive!" she said. Turning away she stepped over to the balcony door and added, "I should think you'd be flattered. And why does it have to stop?"

Dylan wondered what went on in the cobwebbed rooms of Dianna's mind as she was growing up, where her innocence now lay tarnished and abandoned, collecting dust. "*You* know what I mean, Dianna."

"Maybe I'm expecting too much too soon; maybe I'm expecting you to respond too fast." She drained the last of her wine and tossed the glass over her shoulder. It tumbled end-over-end past the railing and down into the street.

Dylan heard a faint tinkling sound as the glass hit the pavement below.

Dianna slipped her shoes back on, then walked quickly past Dylan and on into the kitchen. At the door she turned to face him. "I'll be seeing you soon, Dylan. *Think* about *us*." Opening the door, she took one step onto the darkened landing, then called back as an afterthought. "Oh, you should probably be careful. I told Matthias of my feelings for you . . . and he's awfully jealous."

Through the open kitchen door, Dylan watched her disappear down the stairwell, her shoes making a hollow click-click all the way down the wooden steps.

"I think maybe all the psychiatrists in South Louisiana couldn't do nothing for that girl," Romano observed sagely. He was intent on placing the bottled Cokes into his cooler one by one, as Dylan pulled them out of the case and handed them to him.

A cold, clammy feeling had taken hold of Dylan after Dianna clicked her way downstairs and out into the night. He had felt a desperate need for human companionship and had gone down to the grocery for a visit with Romano. "You may be right about that," Dylan agreed, handing his newfound friend the last of the Cokes.

Romano closed the cooler, wiped his hands on a white handkerchief from his back pocket, and walked back to his stool behind the counter. "I never believed them head doctors did people much good anyway. All that psychosis, neurosis, potty training mumbo jumbo."

"Sounds like you learned something about psychology somewhere."

"My granddaughter's majoring in psychology out at LSU-NO." Romano began taking the bills out of the cash register, counting them, and adding the totals to his daily tally sheet.

"How's she like it?"

Romano shrugged and answered, "Okay, I guess. She tried to explain some of that stuff, but it didn't make any sense to me." He slipped a paper band around the first stack of bills and stuffed them into his Hibernia Bank bag.

"Never did much for me, either," Dylan admitted.

"You know what the difference is between a *psychotic* and a *neurotic?*"

"Beats me," Dylan said. His mind shuffled labels and definitions around like cards, but he decided that Romano's explanation would probably make more sense than the theories and transient truths of his college professors.

Romano counted a stack of tens, licking his thumb with every fourth or fifth bill. "A psychotic says, 'Two plus two is really five,' and a neurotic says, 'No, two plus two is four . . . but it *sure* makes me nervous.' "

Dylan grinned at Romano, who was still counting his tens, then laughed out loud. "That just may be the *best* definition since Freud decided that misery is the only sure sign of an emotionally healthy human being."

"How did we ever get along before the shrinks decided we couldn't get along with out them?" Romano asked as he finished the tens and started on twenties.

"Is there anything *else* I can give you a hand with?"

Romano shook his head and said, "I'm just gonna finish checking out the register and head on home."

"Think I'll call it a night then," Dylan stated. He placed his empty Coke bottle into a wood case at the end of the counter and headed for the door.

"Come on down in the morning for coffee," Romano called out as Dylan left the store.

Climbing the stairs, Dylan could barely smell the aroma of Dianna's perfume, a faint reminder of her visit. He walked into the kitchen and locked the door behind him. The street lamps beyond the balcony bathed the apartment in pale yellow light. Walking on into the living room, he lay down on the couch, resting his head on the pillow from the bed, which had become a permanent addition to this piece of furniture.

Lying in the murky dimness of the room, Dylan let his mind wrap around the events of the past few days. He felt that he had accomplished nothing that would stop the rapidly increasing body count of South Louisiana mayors. The New Orleans Police Department had become his adversary rather than his ally and had probably persuaded the entire task force to join them by this time. *If they want to let Dianna and Teague run free, what can I do to stop them? Tomorrow I pack it in and go home.*

The noise out in the street had dwindled to an occasional yelp of laughter or the sound of tires humming along on the pavement. Dylan stretched out on the couch, letting his muscles relax, willing himself toward sleep.

A few seconds later he thought someone had pressed a baseball glove against his face, then realized it was a giant hand. Lifted bodily, he felt a massive arm grip him around the chest, pressing all the air from his lungs. He tried to gulp air in, but his nose and mouth were pressed tightly shut by the huge, hard hand. Blackness like a gigantic carrion bird swept up and covered him in its cold, smothering grip.

No feeling there at all. What happened? Somebody cut my arms off! No — I can barely feel them now. They're tied beneath my back.

The grass rope cut into Dylan's ankles as

it pulled him toward the foot of the couch. Its twin, looped beneath his armpits, pulled his shoulders toward the opposite end. A thick cloth stuffed into his mouth was held tightly in place by a short length of rope tied behind his head.

Dylan slowly opened his eyes. The kitchen light was on. Dianna's wine bottle sat on the table. In the bulb's harsh glare, Teague, wearing his Camelot outfit complete with soft deerhide moccasins on his wide flat feet, sat at the table. A leather sheath held a big knife at his side. The slim wine glass in his huge hand looked as though it had come from a child's playroom.

Attempting to shift his body off his twisted arms, Dylan made a muffled grunt behind the gag.

Teague turned his head slowly toward the couch, his cropped white hair gleaming in the light. He looked at Dylan with his not-quite-colorless turquoise eyes.

Dylan shivered, in spite of all he could do to stop it, when Teague looked at him. He felt like something that had to be cleaned up off the kitchen floor.

Dylan watched Teague turn away, sipping his wine as though he sat there all alone with all the time in the world. When he had finished his glass of wine, Teague pushed his chair back, stood up, and walked slowly and deliberately into the living room. Sitting on the edge of the couch, he gazed down, his eyes not quite registering any human emotion. Dylan looked into their pale depths with a terror far greater than the fear he had felt gazing into the black depths of the shotgun barrels.

Teague grabbed Dylan's shirt with both hands, then pulled it slowly apart, ripping the buttons off and exposing bare skin. He gripped the stag haft of the heavy knife, sliding it gently from its sheath. The light from the streetlamp hit the long, curved blade with a malignant glint. Dylan struggled against the ropes that bound him, but their taut, unrelenting pull from both ends of his body held him fast.

Sitting back straight as a board, Teague held the knife loosely in his right hand, letting the sharp tip of the blade rest in the hollow of Dylan's throat. A drop of blood formed around the point. Then the big man pulled the knife slowly toward him, letting the dull side of its blade slowly trace a line from Dylan's throat down across his breastbone to his navel.

Dylan fought against the overwhelming horror that faced him, struggling to get enough air down into his lungs. He caught a movement in the kitchen's glare. Above Teague's left shoulder, he watched the top of the door move slowly inward.

Suddenly, Teague's shirt leaped outward as though a puff of wind had blown through a hole in his chest . . . but it remained erect from his body like a small tent with a sharp-tipped center pole. His eyes widened, then slowly drained of light. He placed his knife carefully on Dylan's stomach, leaned side-ways and toppled off the couch onto the floor.

13

Alice and the White Rabbit

Dylan sat on a slick metal bench built into
the concrete-block wall of the holding cell.
Very bright lights were recessed into the ceiling behind heavy wire mesh; an iron door
with a narrow slit at eye-level enclosed the
windowless, airless cell, which reeked with
the smells of unwashed bodies, urine, and
fear.

The lock clicked, the door opened, and
Carbelli stepped inside. He wore a charcoal-
colored duplicate of his brown pinstripe suit,
complete with an identical dazzling white
shirt and burgundy-and-gray striped tie.
"We checked out your story. There may be
a possibility that you *didn't* kill Teague."

"A possibility?" Dylan stood up, still wearing his wrinkled khakis and the shirt Teague
had ripped apart. He held out his wrists,
rubbed raw from the tight rope. "You see
this? It took me three hours to finally cut
myself loose with that maniac's knife." His

voice rumbled with anger. "You think I shot him, got rid of the crossbow, tied myself up tight enough to do this, cut the ropes with his knife, and then called the police?"

Carbelli rubbed the back of his neck with his left hand. "Maybe you're right. I guess the boys got a little . . . *overzealous* when they cuffed you and locked you back here."

"Overzealous! Is *that* what they were?" Dylan felt himself on the brink of losing control. Taking a deep breath, he settled down. He knew the one thing that men in positions of public trust feared when they had done something illegal or merely stupid was the press. "Do you think some *overzealous* reporter *might* find this is an . . . interesting story? A cop arrested for the murder of a lunatic who tried to kill him, even though a blind monkey could see he didn't do it!"

"Follow me," Carbelli ordered. He turned and walked out.

Dylan followed him down a dimly lit passageway, through a metal door, and out into a bright hall with dark paneling. Three doors down, they turned into Carbelli's office.

"Hi, Dylan," Dianna's smile was as bright as Carbelli's teeth. She sat in the chair to the left of his desk, wearing her parochial girl's school costume: green plaid skirt, white cotton blouse with a Peter Pan collar, and brown penny loafers.

Dylan found himself staring at her, speechless, thinking absurdly that the three of them might soon be leaving for an "un-birthday party" with Alice and the White Rabbit.

Carbelli walked around his desk and sat down. "Won't you have a seat, Mr. St. John?" he invited.

Mr. St. John? This man is definitely afraid I'll make trouble for him.

Pulling the chair five inches to the right, Dylan sat down, glancing at Dianna's now demure posture; feet planted together in front of the chair, skirt smoothed primly over her knees, hands folded on her lap.

Clearing his throat, Carbelli spoke in an officious voice, pronouncing his words very precisely. "Miss Salazar has graciously come forward in your defense."

Dylan merely nodded his head, as yet unable to comprehend what was happening between Carbelli and Dianna. His mind kept flashing on Teague and his big knife.

Carbelli nodded toward Dylan. "Aren't you the *least* bit interested?"

"I don't understand what's going on here," Dylan openly admitted, realizing that it was a little late in the game to start a verbal fencing match with the two of them, especially since they had the home court advantage.

Dianna spoke to Carbelli, "I just couldn't let Dyl — Mr. St. John take the blame for . . ." she turned toward Dylan, noticing the dark bead of clotted blood clinging to the base of his throat. "Oh, goodness, *you're hurt!*"

Dylan touched the tiny ball, plucked it with his fingertips, and tossed it on the floor.

Carbelli winced. "He's fine, Dianna."

She frowned at a fresh droplet of blood forming on Dylan's neck, then said, "Well, I just couldn't let an innocent man take the blame for — for, well you both know *what for*."

A thought finally penetrated the vaporous dark that seemed to surround Dylan's mind. He turned toward Dianna and asked, "How did you find out about Teague?"

Dianna opened her mouth, but Carbelli's voice answered the question. "*I* called her."

"I only reported Teague's injuries two hours ago, and she's already in your office. Is *that* standard procedure?"

"I knew that Teague was a close friend of Miss Salazar's, so I called her shortly after I found out." Carbelli seemed pleased with the way things were going. "At first she was reluctant to say anything, but she finally admitted that Teague had threatened you in her presence."

"She did?" Dylan could make no sense of the bizarre twistings and turnings his life had taken since coming to New Orleans. *Now she's defending me!* "Well, I guess *I* wasn't in my presence when he threatened me because *I* certainly don't remember it."

A look of mild shock crossed Carbelli's face. "I don't understand you at all, Mr. St. —"

"Dylan."

"What?"

"Lay off the 'Mr. St. John,' will you?"

"Sure." Carbelli straightened his already neatly knotted tie and continued. "Now, as I was saying, Miss Salazar is coming to your defense, and you seem to be fighting against it. No, I'm afraid I don't understand that at all."

What's the use? These people are all nuts — either that, or maybe I am. He looked at Carbelli, poised, in control; then at Dianna, a picture of innocence. *Here we are in the district commander's office and this insane girl is running the whole show.*

"Well?"

Dylan knew he didn't need anyone to come to his defense; that no DA in the state would accept the charges, even if Carbelli

264

were foolish enough to file them. Then, in a sudden revelation, he realized that as long as Dianna kept herself in the game he still had a chance to stop her from killing again. *Unless of course Dianna had merely been along for the kicks and Teague had been the killer all along, but now Teague was out of the picture.* He decided that fighting the insanity was useless; better to drift along with the flow of it and see where it took him.

"Well?" Carbelli repeated, his hands pressed together, forming a steeple in front of his chin.

"I'm an ingrate."

"What?"

Dylan turned toward Dianna, forcing a half-smile onto his face. "Thanks for your help."

"You're welcome."

"Well, now that we've taken care of that little matter," Carbelli said, sounding like a parish priest who had just settled a spat between two third-graders, "does anybody want coffee?"

Dylan decided to buck the flow briefly. "Where does this leave Teague's murder?"

Carbelli smiled. "We're already working on it. I never really thought it was you, if you want to know the truth. It's just standard procedure to turn the heat on anybody who's present when a crime is committed . . . see how they react."

"*That's* a real comfort."

Carbelli actually laughed, then cut it off after three quarters of a second. Glancing from Dianna to Dylan, he said, "I take it no one wants coffee then?"

"I'd like to go home and change clothes," Dylan said. He glanced down at his shirt, hanging in tatters.

Carbelli opened his middle desk drawer and handed Dylan the automatic.

Standing up, Dylan took the pistol and stuck it in his waistband at the small of his back.

"I'd be happy to give you a ride," Dianna offered, still seated in her schoolgirl pose.

Flow with it. "I'd appreciate that."

She gave him a victory smile.

Dianna gripped the steering wheel of Teague's big Ford pickup, turning right off Canal onto St. Charles Avenue.

"This is *not* the way to my apartment, Dianna." Dylan looked through the windshield at the streetcar swaying along in the busy traffic.

"I want to show you my home."

"Maybe later." Dylan found himself undergoing a delayed reaction to his being treated like a criminal by Carbelli. He fought against the anger, knowing it would produce nothing but a cluttered mind. What he needed was reasoning power. "Right now I've got to get out of these rags."

Dianna maneuvered the pickup like a covered wagon through the traffic. "You can put on some of Daddy's old clothes. He's got plenty."

Dylan gazed at the crowded sidewalks, clogged with people hurrying about the business of living. He had already forgotten what a life of order and routine felt like, the eight-to-five office schedule with lunch and two coffee breaks. Once he had despised the sameness of it; now he wasn't so sure.

"You all right?" Dianna asked, her brow furrowing as she glanced at Dylan.

Dylan assumed the question was academic and changed to another subject. "How'd you get Teague's truck?" He considered the absurdity of Dianna's driving the pickup of the man she had arguably just murdered.

"He let me keep it sometimes when he didn't have any need for it." Dianna appeared as cool as a first frost, not quite smiling as she continued, "He didn't have any family, and he obviously doesn't need a truck now."

"His death doesn't seem to bother you

very much," Dylan said, hoping to open a niche in Dianna's seamless armor plating. "Wasn't he a good friend?"

"He was . . . an acquaintance. I guess that's as close as I could put him in my life." She left St. Charles, barely missing a street-car crossing the intersection, drove past Prytania, and turned onto Coliseum.

"Do your acquaintances *usually* get jealous enough to try to kill for you?"

"It wasn't for me."

"Poor choice of words," Dylan said, although it occurred to him that it may have been precisely correct. "*Because* of you then. Is that better?"

"Matthias was crazy."

Sensing somehow that this was as far as he would get in the matter of Dianna's relationship with Teague, Dylan let it go.

Dianna made a U-turn, pulled over to the curb, and parked next to a bronze plaque designating the house as being a National Historic Landmark.

Dylan gazed at the three-story house rising behind the scrolled and feathered iron fence. Getting out of the truck, he followed Dianna up the brick walkway onto the gallery, around to the left, and through a side entrance into a foyer.

"This is where I used to play," Dianna

said, continuing on through the foyer.

Dylan followed Dianna on a tour of all three floors of the house. Old and elegant, constructed with heart cypress floors, dark paneling, and beaded crown molding, it possessed a foreboding quality like that of a mausoleum someone had furnished with expensive antiques.

After refusing a change of clothes from the mayor's extensive wardrobe, Dylan was left on his own while Dianna went back to the kitchen to make coffee. He wandered back to the foyer where they had first come into the house. An alcove beneath the stairs caught his eye. He walked over, pulled aside a curtain, and saw the world of the child Dianna Salazar had been — maybe still was.

An exquisite doll dressed in handmade clothes sat in a chair at a toy table set with a china tea service. The doll had been lovely once, but the torn sockets where its eyes had been now gave it a grotesque appearance. A bookshelf against the wall held volumes of the tales of Camelot, the traditional and legendary home of King Arthur and his Knights of the Round Table.

Dylan sat on the floor of the tiny alcove, thumbing through the books with their colorful bindings and pictures of knights errant riding to adventure; tournaments and high festivals; Arthur marrying Guinevere in the church of St. Stephens; the Grail brought into the presence of the assembled knights.

"You like my playhouse?" Dianna asked as she handed Dylan a delicate flowered cup with a silver rim, then sat down next to him, crossing her legs.

"I imagine you spent a lot of time here in Camelot when you were a girl."

Dianna looked into the distance toward a land only she could see. "Where all the men were handsome and noble and pure, and their maidens were innocent and faithful."

Dylan sipped his coffee. "Sounds like you're still hoping to find a world like that."

"I used to think that one day my knight in shining armor would come and carry me away from this house," Dianna said with a sigh. "To Camelot or some place very much like that." She glanced at Dylan, then stared into her cup. "But of course he never did."

"I guess they all died with Arthur in Camelot," Dylan mumbled distractedly. He thought of Dianna growing up in this old and elegant home that held not one touch of human warmth.

Dianna turned her head slightly upward, gazing at Dylan with longing eyes. "*You* could be my knight, Dylan." Her voice had softened, the words sibilant in the hushed room. "*You've* proven yourself faithful and true."

Dylan realized in disbelief where the current of Dianna's thoughts were carrying them. "I don't think I understand what you're saying."

"You had all the chances in the world with me, and you remained faithful to your wife. I believe you're the one to take me away from this dreadful place."

"But don't you see," Dylan said with a barely concealed urgency, "if I did that, I'd no longer be faithful."

Dianna ignored the obvious logic of his statement. "We could be married," she smiled placidly, "and I'd make you the most wonderful wife — I promise."

Dylan tried to end the insanity that was engulfing their conversation. "Dianna, you didn't have the right to execute those men, just because they were unfaithful to their wives. Don't you see that?"

The smile slipped from Dianna's face. "Men like *that* don't *deserve* to live. Believe me, I know."

Staring into her face as she spoke, Dylan saw a dramatic change. Just for moment, a veil seemed to lift from her eyes . . . they looked as old as tombs. "The world isn't like Camelot, Dianna," he said softly, holding out one of her books. "No one is perfectly noble and pure."

Light glittered in Dianna's eyes. "You're turning me away . . . just like — you don't want anything to do with me. I'm mean and ugly . . . that's what you really think, isn't it?"

"Dianna, settle down! Let me get you some help!" Dylan could think of no clear way to defuse the situation. Dianna's mind had gone very wrong sometime long ago, and he could see that there would be no easy or short way back. "You don't have to live like this anymore."

"It's not me!" She almost shrieked. "It's this *dirty* world . . . and the *dirty* people in it."

Dylan knew for a certainty at that moment, that as long as Dianna kept longing and looking for Camelot, she would never stop killing the men who didn't measure up to its perfect and unattainable ideals. "You can't change the world, Dianna. You can only change yourself."

"I can think of *one* change that would make the world a far better place." Her eyes glinted like mica. "And it's a change only *I* can make." She leaped to her feet, spilling her coffee and ran for the front door.

"Dianna!" Dylan scrambled up to follow

her, but she had already gained the gallery and was headed for the front walk. He ran after her, watching her fly down the brick walk, out the gate, and leap into the truck. She pushed the locks down on both doors and started the engine.

From the sidewalk, Dylan shouted after her, "Dianna! You've got to end this!"

Dianna stared at him through the driver's side window, a look of hopeless resignation in her eyes, and mouthed the words, "It's too late." She slammed the truck into gear and shot forward, the tires screeching against the blacktop, laying down twin paths of burnt rubber as the truck fishtailed out into the street.

Dylan watched her speed away in the big truck, turn left at the end of the block, and vanish behind a white-columned house on the corner.

"Was that Dianna?"

Turning around, Dylan saw him — the man who had presented his tennis trophy so long ago — strolling casually down the brick walkway. He was shorter than Dylan remembered and wore a wine-colored blazer, gray pleated slacks, and glossy black shoes. And he had stamped Dianna's features indelibly with his own. Looking at him, Dylan couldn't imagine that Dianna had favored her mother at all.

"Yes sir."

Stopping at the gate, Salazar gave Dylan the once-over. "I don't believe I know you. Are you a friend of Dianna's?"

From that first question, Dylan knew it was going to be a difficult conversation, but one that he must have with Dianna's father. "I need to talk with you, Mayor. Maybe we could go in the house."

With a skeptical glance at Dylan's torn shirt, held together by two buttons, Salazar reluctantly agreed. "I'm rather pressed for time, but if it's something to do with my daughter's welfare, then I'll give you a few moments."

"It is."

Dylan followed Salazar back toward the house, through the foyer, and into his study. Salazar sat down behind his massive rosewood desk and ushered Dylan into a brown leather chair across from him. Dylan felt awkward, his knees above the level of his waist in the shortened chair, allowing Salazar to look down on him . . . or anyone else he brought into his study.

Heavy, dark furniture and bookcases blended tastefully with the drapes of a burnished gold color. Two brass floor lamps gave the room the soft amber glow of per-

274

petual twilight. Photographs and other memorabilia documented Salazar's thirty-plus years in the Louisiana political arena.

"I have an idea your name is St. John." Salazar gazed down on Dylan as though he were a supplicant come to bring him an offering. "Am I right?"

"Yes sir." Dylan could just imagine where Carbelli had learned his posturing.

Thinking that he was probably raising this particular exercise in futility to the level of an art form, Dylan launched into the same story of Dianna as Camelot Killer that he had related to the New Orleans Police, ending with Damon Carbelli. He had hardly begun when Salazar stopped him.

"That's enough." The mayor held his hands up in protest, like a referee giving Dylan a penalty. "Lieutenant Carbelli told me what to expect out of you. I just wanted to hear some of it for myself to make sure he wasn't exaggerating. It's obvious that he wasn't."

In a way, Dylan felt relieved that he didn't have to finish his bizarre-sounding tale. "I thought you might react like this, Mayor, but for your own safety, I felt obligated to tell you what I know about your daughter."

"You mean what you *suspect* about her, don't you?"

"No, I was merely telling you the facts so you could draw your own conclusions," Dylan said flatly. "What I *suspect* is that you're the next intended victim."

Salazar appeared mildly stunned by Dylan's words, then his expression changed and he threw back his head and laughed. "Me, the next victim — and at the hands of my own daughter? Carbelli understated your mental condition, Mr. St. John. You're positively certifiable."

Again, Dylan fought the anger welling up inside him. "I haven't had a very nice time in your city, Mayor. I haven't been treated very well at all." He continued, speaking slowly and calmly. "Apparently you, as well as everyone in your entire police department, are incapable of seeing what's happening here."

"You're talking about my daughter."

"I understand that, but you're totally ignoring the possibility of her being involved — in spite of the evidence."

Salazar folded his hands, placing them on the desk. "Do you really think that Dianna would display her skills with the crossbow in full view of the whole city if she were involved in these bizarre killings?"

"Yes I do."

"Why?"

"Because she believes that she's above the law . . . that it can't touch her." Staring at Salazar's smug expression, Dylan felt he knew the birthplace of Dianna's beliefs. "And so far, she's been proven totally right."

"Look, Mr. St. John, I'm going to be perfectly honest with you." Salazar took his perfectly honest mask out of his closet of expressions and put it on. "My daughter has been quite a handful at times. Speeding tickets, drunk and disorderly. She even took a car and went joyriding once — unauthorized use of a movable, they called it — but what you're considering is unthinkable. She could never be involved in something like that."

"You're her father. I understand that."

Salazar glanced at his watch. "Look, I've run out of time. Have to make some presentations down at City Hall in an hour and a half. I'm sure you can find your own way out." He stood up, gazing directly into Dylan's eyes. "One more thing — *you've* run out of time, too."

"I don't understand."

"I'd take it as a personal favor if you'd make this your last night in my city — for a long while." He abruptly left the room.

Dylan knew all too well the import of the words *my city*. He sat in Salazar's plush and comfortable study, wondering how much time the man had left to live. Suddenly it occurred to him that this afternoon's speech might possibly be his last. Leaving the house, he walked the two blocks over to St. Charles Avenue and after a ten-minute wait took a streetcar toward the Quarter.

14

Love Letters

After a shower as cold as he could stand it, Dylan felt as though he had reentered the land of the living. His body craved sleep, but that would have to wait. He put on his boots, Levi's, and a khaki shirt with the tail hanging out to hide the .45. Then he left the apartment, walked the three blocks to where the Blazer was parked, and fought his way through the rush-hour traffic to Poydras Plaza. As the downtown was now emptying, he found a parking place in the public lot across from City Hall.

Dylan sat in the Blazer, keeping watch for Teague's red Ford pickup. Thirty minutes later, Salazar, accompanied by two uniformed policemen, walked over to a squat podium set up in front of City Hall. Several trophies adorned a table next to it. A small group of people, waiting for him in two short rows of folding chairs, stood up and applauded. A listless newsman, his camera slung on his shoulder, leaned against the building scribbling on a notepad. The mayor unfolded a sheet of paper, placed it on the podium, and began to speak to the dozen or so onlookers.

As he got out of the Blazer, Dylan scanned the plaza area. He checked Loyola Avenue and LaSalle and Poydras Streets, and finally the three approaches to the front of the building. Glancing back toward the mayor, he saw one of the policemen handing him a tall trophy, gleaming as the late sunlight struck its polished gold surface. As Salazar took it, a slim blonde boy standing at his left smiled at the prize he was about to receive.

Suddenly, Dylan saw a flicking motion in his left periphery. The bolt from the crossbow had already reached the apex of its arc and was hurtling downward toward the mayor. A fraction of a second later, the trophy flew from the mayor's hand, bouncing on the marble landing, then tumbled down the steps, the bolt embedded deep into its gleaming side.

Dylan saw her then, walking in no apparent hurry from behind a white Irwin's Florist van parked in the Girod Street lot across the Plaza. She still had on her schoolgirl outfit, but had discarded her weapon. As she disappeared behind the post office, Dylan gunned the Blazer out into Loyola's still-heavy traffic and lurched around the corner onto Girod.

As he accelerated toward the end of the block, Dylan saw the driver of the florist's van walk across from the post office into the parking lot, bend down, and pick up the crossbow. Wheeling into the entrance, Dylan braked to a stop, leaned over, and opened the passenger-side door. "Give me that thing!"

The driver stared wide-eyed from behind his tiny gold-rimmed glasses. "What?"

Dylan fumbled his badge out of his pocket and shoved it toward the driver. "Give it here."

"I didn't know it was yours. Don't shoot me!" The stunned driver took two steps forward, one hand in the air, the other holding the crossbow out at arm's length.

Taking it by the string, Dylan looped it onto the floorboard. "What's your name?"

"Vernon."

"Remember this." Dylan slammed the door, shrieked around in a U-turn, and gunned the Blazer toward the corner where Dianna had disappeared. Turning left, he saw her behind the wheel of the red pickup, barreling up the Claiborne entrance ramp onto I-10. Following her, Dylan pulled out into the thinning stream of traffic flowing out of downtown toward the suburbs.

Dylan had little trouble keeping up with the red pickup. Dianna appeared to be in no particular hurry, but was driving erratically, swerving abruptly from lane to lane for no apparent reason, braking and accelerating in random patterns. Several times drivers had to pull sharply away to keep her from banging into them. He decided it would be best to keep his distance.

Four or five cars ahead of him, Dianna took the long curve heading west. A few minutes later, she exited onto Causeway Boulevard. Stopping at the Veteran's Boulevard red light, Dylan saw there was only an MG convertible between him and Dianna. He watched her glance into the rearview mirror, recognizing him. She gunned the pickup across the intersection, crashing into the front of a black sedan, then went speeding on down Causeway toward Lake Pontchartrain.

Dylan rolled down his window, plugged the flashing red light into its socket, and slapped it onto the roof of the Blazer. Threading his way through the almost blocked intersection, he kept Dianna in sight. Traveling now at high speed, she weaved in and out of traffic, her brake lights winking on and off.

Picking up speed, Dylan considered calling State Police for back-up, then discarded the thought. NOPD, monitoring the band, would dispatch their own units. He pictured his Blazer forced off the road, his arms pinned behind his back, wrists thrust into handcuffs, while Dianna drove away as untouched as her father had been by the iron-tipped bolt from her crossbow.

Soon Dylan saw palm trees rising against the lavender sky, then the wind-torn, slate-green surface of the lake. Shrimpers chugged toward the harbor, their work finished for the day. Sailboats cut through the whitecaps, canvas sails slapping in the wind. Far off to the left, a twin-engine cabin cruiser, its white superstructure gleaming in the last sunlight, churned toward the causeway.

Ahead of him, Dylan could see traffic backed up at the tollbooth. Dianna suddenly jerked the red pickup out of the line, rushing toward a closed-off lane at the approach to the bridge. Dylan pulled out to the side of the long line, chasing her, his red light flashing. He saw her accelerating, the pickup bouncing, lurching from side to side. Then she lost it.

The left front of the grill slammed into the concrete barrier that housed the tollgate.

The pickup lifted in the rear, then careened crazily to the side, plowing with a shrieking and tearing of metal into a bronze-colored Oldsmobile '98 blocking the line of traffic.

Dylan saw Dianna fighting with the door handle of the pickup, then slam her shoulder against it, forcing it open. She slid off the seat, holding to the side of the truck for balance. Blood streamed from a cut above her right eye. Dazed, she looked around and saw Dylan stop the Blazer twenty yards away. Reaching back into the truck, she pulled a knife from under the seat.

Dylan stepped out of the Blazer. "It's all right, Dianna!" He walked toward her, careful to make no threatening moves. "You're going to be all right."

Around them, people were poking their heads out of car windows, some getting out, staring at the wrecked vehicles, the wounded girl, and the man approaching her. A uniformed attendant in the tollbooth was frantically dialing a telephone. Car horns began sounding far back in the line.

Dianna shook her head back and forth slowly. "No . . . I'm *not* going to be all right."

"Put the knife down, Dianna!" Dylan ordered. He recognized it as the same one Teague had used, or one just like it.

Glancing once at the gawking onlookers, Dianna turned toward Dylan, a strange, sad, pleading smile on her face. Then she sprinted past the toll gate onto the causeway. Southbound travelers slowing for the tollbooth stared wide-eyed at the young woman, dressed like a schoolgirl, carrying a very large grown-up knife as she ran past them in the north lanes.

Dylan ran after her, trying to keep her close without catching her, well aware of the hard, lethal presence of the .45 pressing against the base of his spine. Off to his left he glanced at the huge, red flattened rim of the sun burning on the far edge of the lake.

Then he saw them skimming across the water toward the bridge, thousands and thousands of purple martins. Flying close together, they swirled upward over the bridge like a huge dark cloud, the last rays of sunlight shattering on their gleaming wings.

Turning again toward Dianna, he saw her slowing down as the birds banked west again, this time flying low over the bridge directly toward her. She ran west across the roadway into the red glowing sunset, stopping at the railing. Ahead of her far out over the water, another great black cloud came swooping across the black-green surface of the lake.

Dianna spun around, her back against the

railing, slashing at the birds in the air with her big knife. A third flight soared high above the causeway, then banked into a headlong dive toward the water. Great clouds of birds filled the purple twilight under, over, and around the bridge, swooping and swirling in their nightly ritual.

In the eerie, fluttering sound of thousands upon thousands of wings beating the air, Dylan walked toward Dianna. Behind her, through the swirling birds, he saw the big cruiser plowing the dark water. Its skipper and his three passengers were totally absorbed with the skies about them.

Suddenly, Dianna began screaming.

Dylan walked toward her. "Dianna! Dianna! It's all right. It's all right!" He could not imagine what dark chamber in her mind filled her with such terror at the sound and sight of the birds. "Put the knife down and walk toward me."

Her face twisted with fear, Dianna climbed backward over the rail, standing on the outside edge of the roadway. She hurled the knife into the air. Tumbling end over end, it disappeared beyond the far railing.

Dylan stared at her, a corona of red light outlining her dark, wind-ruffled hair. He suddenly realized that she was trying to climb down beneath the bridge to get away from the swarms of birds all around her. He pictured thousands of them settling down for the night on the cross beams just beneath the bridge. "Dianna, stop! Don't go down there!"

She ducked beneath the railing, one hand still grasping it, then turned loose and vanished over the edge.

Dylan ran across the roadway to the railing. As he leaned over, peering down into the black shadows beneath the bridge, he heard a great muffled beating of wings, then an agonizing, piercing scream.

Dianna tumbled backward, downward, toward the water, breaking the surface in front of the cruiser's prow. Dylan looked directly downward at the front deck, then at the cabin's roof, and then at the wide rear deck with its captain and crew still watching the airshow of the purple martins. As the boat disappeared beneath the bridge, Dylan stared down through the violet air at the churning, swirling wake, that had taken on the color of the afterglow in the western sky.

"I know you want to get on home," Emile said, tapping a pencil end over end on his desktop, "but this couldn't wait."

A deep weariness had settled over Dylan on his drive up from New Orleans; a weariness more of the soul than the body. He gazed at Emile's jaw muscles working beneath the taut skin; unmistakable sadness in those dark eyes . . . and he knew. "It's about Remy."

Emile nodded, placing the pencil carefully aside. "The FBI called this afternoon."

Dylan slumped in a chair next to the desk.

"He's been taken out of the country. The others, too." Emile's voice dropped barely above a whisper. "They . . . and the Bureau wouldn't say who . . . were operating in several states. Sending children into North Africa through Tunis and Tripoli and to a couple of the Mideast oil kingdoms. They're shut down now."

"No way to —"

"None at all, Dylan. It's international. The Bureau's working through the State Department now, but don't get your hopes up. They never have much luck with countries in that part of the world."

Dylan felt a cold anger, leaning toward rage. "You sure they're not just trying to get us to lay off. Maybe —"

"No," Emile interrupted. "I've known this agent for a long time. He plays it straight. Probably why they got him to make the call to me."

"But why? Why take children?"

Emile shifted in his chair. "It started in India. *They* sent representatives there promising parents they'd give their children a better life. Since they were starving at home, some of the parents gave in . . . thought it was the best thing they could do for their kids. Then these *people* used them for entertainment . . . in camel races."

Dylan shook his head, trying to grasp Emile's meaning.

"They'd use the children as riders. They'd start the race, then the kids would be terrified and start crying, scaring the camels who would run faster and . . . well, you get the picture. That was one story . . . you don't want to hear any more.

"Then they started branching out to other countries. Finally got around to us."

Dylan leaned forward, elbows on his knees, staring down at the scuffed tile floor.

Standing up, Emile walked over to the window and gazed out at the darkened street. "Absolute power; unlimited supply of money; and all the time in the world. That's a bad combination."

Dylan fought against the weariness and the darkness that had begun to cloud his mind. He knew now with absolute certainty there was nothing left to do. "Don't tell Susan."

"Sure."

"I'll talk to her about it after the baby comes." Standing slowly to his feet he walked over to the door.

"Dylan . . ."

"Yeah." He turned, leaning one hand on the doorframe.

"Don't take this home with you. Leave it right here in this office."

Dylan stared at Emile for a long time, then slowly nodded his head. "I'll try."

"That's a strange, strange story, sweetheart," Susan said. Wearing white shorts and a pink cotton top, she sat on the plank decking of the boat dock, Dylan's head resting in her lap. She glanced at the amber glow of her kitchen window, then stared upward at the night's first star winking on in the deep blue sky.

"That girl seemed so determined to die." Dylan thought of the sunset on the causeway the day before, and it seemed like a hundred years ago. "I think she made up her mind as soon as she loosed that arrow at her father."

Dylan felt Susan's soft fingers stroking his face, then their feathery touch trailing down across his shoulders and chest. "She just hadn't decided how she was going to go about it. Maybe she didn't even realize what

290

she was doing there at the end."

"Do you really think she killed those men?" Susan asked.

Dylan considered Dianna's near-perfect shot at the Camelot Festival; her fury turned loose on Teague later that same day next to the lagoon at City Park; the attempt on her own father's life. Then Teague's pale, dead eyes appeared in his mind like a half-forgotten nightmare. "I don't know, Susan. I just don't know." He closed his eyes, savoring the touch of his wife's hands. "I believe Teague was capable of anything — except maybe for common human decency and compassion."

"But what about the Evangeline Festival? You said you saw her running away."

"It *looked* like her," Dylan said, recalling Dianna in her plaid skirt and white blouse, looking about fifteen years old, instead of that shadowy figure running toward Evangeline Bayou, "but I really didn't see her face."

Surprisingly, he discovered that he didn't want to believe Dianna had been capable of such a thing. But then, of course, she was. He had seen her try to kill her own father. What had Salazar done to his daughter all those years ago in that lovely old house on Coliseum Street to make her hate him with such a violent, relentless vengeance? And the others — simply because they were unfaithful to their wives? Or because they wore the label *mayor?*

"What about this Teague? What did he look like?"

Dylan felt a cold stab of fear in his gut as he described the man. "Why do you want to know?"

"He came to the house."

"What?" Dylan held back his reaction to sit up and lecture his wife on the common-sense approach to home safety. Relaxing again, he let her talk.

Susan's voice held no anxiety as she told Dylan of the big white-haired man who came to their house under the pretext of engine trouble. "He didn't seem much of a threat. Actually," she let her hand rest on Dylan's, "I felt kind of sorry for him. He seemed so . . . sad . . . and so lonely."

Dylan felt a single warm tear fall on his shoulder and wondered at the incredible expanse of Susan's heart that could hold pity for a man like Teague.

She continued, her voice slightly shaky. "It was almost like he was the only one of his kind left and there was no place for him to go. I felt that he really didn't know what to do with himself anymore."

"I *hope* he was the last of his kind, but I'm afraid there're a lot more out there." Dylan sat up, turning around and sitting cross-legged in front of Susan. He took both of her hands. "Don't let anybody in the house when I'm gone. Okay?"

Susan nodded.

Dylan brushed her hair with his fingertips. "I think maybe I should show you how to use a pistol."

Shaking her head, Susan said, "I'd probably just shoot myself in the foot."

"You're probably right," Dylan admitted and laughed. Then his voice took on a somber tone. "I think maybe I should do something else. Maybe I could —"

"No. This is a good place to live." Susan cut him off, then gazed into his eyes and squeezed his hands. "We can't live in the shadows, Dylan. We're not going to let fear make the decisions in this marriage."

"Maybe it's just common sense to —"

"No it's not. The only thing that bothers me about Teague is that I didn't have the courage to tell him about Jesus." Susan stared out across the star-filled water. "I was reading Paul's second letter to the church at Corinth . . . he said that each Christian is a letter from Christ, written not on tablets of stone but on human hearts."

She looked deep into Dylan's eyes. "I truly believe that we're meant to be love letters from Jesus to the world . . . and He doesn't exclude people like Teague."

Dylan nodded. "Maybe you're right, but who's going to read a letter under six feet of dirt?"

Susan smiled, her green eyes catching faint starlight. "That makes sense too, I guess. Do you think that Mayor Salazar's really going to resign?"

Dylan found that he was always surprised at Susan's abrupt turnings in the course of their conversations, but he had learned to make the turns with her. "That was on the six o'clock news. Let's see what happens at ten. I've found that politicians occasionally say things they don't really mean."

"You too." Susan took his face in her hands and kissed him on the lips. "Supper in fifteen minutes." Placing her hand on his shoulder for balance, she stood up.

"There's a darkness in this world deeper than people can imagine." He was surprised at his own words. He didn't know they were there, just below the surface of his thoughts, until they came spilling out.

Susan stared at him. "Why'd you say that?"

"I don't know."

"There's a light that shines in the deepest darkness," Susan said, her voice soft as the breeze rustling through the reeds growing at the water's edge. "And I know *exactly* why I said that." She turned, heading across the dock toward the cabin.

Watching her walk away, Dylan's mind turned toward Dianna and her sad and tortured life. He thought of Teague; tried to see him as Susan had: lonely and sad, the only one of his kind left, and no place to go. But the memory of that big knife against his throat made pity as elusive for him as happiness had been for Dianna.

Then a sudden thought stunned him. *I wonder what kind of person I'd be if it weren't for the love letters? Could I have become another Teague? Maybe Dianna's life would have been completely different if she'd been given just one love letter.*

Dylan pondered Susan's brief parable on love letters. She had most certainly been a living love letter to him; his parents and his grandmother had been others. He smiled, thinking that his grandfather was more like a loudspeaker than a letter, but as a child he had taught him the message of that old, old love letter. "For God so loved the world, that he gave his only begotten son, that whosoever believeth in him should not perish, but have everlasting life."

Dylan gazed up at the sky, a deep, deep blue and crowded with stars. The night wind felt cool across his face. He knew one certainty — that he didn't deserve Susan and the happiness she had given him. He smiled at the thought that he now had the good sense to be grateful for her. He thought of the child they would have in the fall. Another love letter in his life. *What world deserves more attention than this?*

7-8